PENGUIN CLASSICS

MANON LESCAUT

Antoine-François Prévost was born in Artois in 1697, the son of a provincial official. Educated by the Jesuits, he entered the army, later returning to the Jesuits. He then rejoined the army, only to abandon a military career for a life of austerity as a Benedictine monk with the congregation of Saint-Maur. However, his taste for a worldly life and his doubts about his vocation led him, in 1728, to flee the cloister. He spent the next six years in exile in Holland and England, returning to France in 1734. His arduous literary career began in 1728 with his first romance, *Mémoires d'un homme de qualité*, followed in 1731–9 by *Le Philosophe anglais ou les mémoires de M. Cleveland*, a romance of love and adventure, which showed in germ some of the ideas later found in Rousseau's political philosophy. His greatest work is undoubtedly *Manon Lescaut*, the publication of which in 1731 caused a sensation and it was ordered to be seized. Despite this it was an enormous success. Prévost spent the next twenty years occupied with several novels, vast compilations, such as an *Histoire générale des voyages*, and with translations of Richardson's novels. These translations helped to promote the knowledge of English literature in France. Prévost died in 1763, of an attack of apoplexy.

Leonard Tancock spent most of his life in or near London, apart from a year as a student in Paris, most of the Second World War in Wales and three periods in American universities as visiting professor. Until his death in 1986, he was a Fellow of University College, London, and was formerly Reader in French at the University. He prepared his first Penguin Classic in 1949 and, from that time, was extremely interested in the problems of translation, about which he wrote, lectured and gave broadcasts. His numerous translations for the Penguin Classics include Zola's *Germinal*, *Thérèse Raquin*, *The Débâcle*, *L'Assommoir* and *La Bête Humaine*; Diderot's *The Nun*, *Rameau's Nephew* and *D'Alembert's Dream*; Maupassant's *Pierre and Jean*; Marivaux's *Up from the Country*; Constant's *Adolphe*; La Rochefoucauld's *Maxims*; Voltaire's *Letters on England*; and Madame de Sévigné's *Selected Letters*.

Jean Sgard is Professor of French Literature at the Stendhal University in Grenoble. He studied in Paris and has held various positions at the universities of Göteborg (in Sweden), Paris and Lyon. He has written several works on Prévost, *Prévost romancier* (1968 and 1989), *Le Pour et Contre de Prévost* (1972) and *L'Abbé Prévost: les labyrinthes de la mémoire* (1984), and is General Editor of the definitive edition of the works of Prévost (eight volumes, University of Grenoble Press). He has also written numerous articles on the seventeenth and eighteenth centuries and is the General Editor of *Dictionnaire de la presse (1600–1789)*.

ABBÉ PRÉVOST

Manon Lescaut

Translated by
LEONARD TANCOCK

with a new Introduction and Notes by
JEAN SGARD

PENGUIN BOOKS

PENGUIN BOOKS

Published by the Penguin Group
Penguin Books Ltd, 80 Strand, London WC2R ORL, England
Penguin Group (USA) Inc., 375 Hudson Street, New York, New York 10014, USA
Penguin Books Australia Ltd, 250 Camberwell Road, Camberwell, Victoria 3124, Australia
Penguin Books Canada Ltd, 10 Alcorn Avenue, Toronto, Ontario, Canada M4V 3B2
Penguin Books India (P) Ltd, 11 Community Centre, Panchsheel Park, New Delhi – 110 017, India
Penguin Group (NZ), cnr Airborne and Rosedale Roads, Albany, Auckland 1310, New Zealand
Penguin Books (South Africa) (Pty) Ltd, 24 Sturdee Avenue, Rosebank 2196, South Africa

Penguin Books Ltd, Registered Offices: 80 Strand, London WC2R ORL, England

www.penguin.com

First published in Penguin Books 1949
Second edition, with Introduction and Notes by Jean Sgard, 1991
Reprinted with corrections and a Chronology 2004

15

Copyright 1949 by Leonard Tancock
Introduction, notes and Chronology copyright © Jean Sgard 1991, 2004

Printed in England by Clays Ltd, St Ives plc

CONTENTS

INTRODUCTION

Amsterdam 1731

This short novel, which was to create such a stir, was probably written in the course of a few weeks in an Amsterdam inn at the beginning of 1731. No evidence has survived as to its genesis and publication. We know that Prévost returned from England in October 1730 and that in November, in Amsterdam, he was anxious to secure his future by signing several publishing contracts – notably for *Cleveland*, a somewhat ambitious novel, two volumes of which he had already completed and which he was trying hard to finish off quickly by the end of the year. His Dutch publishers, on the other hand, were hoping for a sequel to the *Mémoires et aventures d'un homme de qualité*, four volumes of which had appeared in 1728–9 with resounding success.

Three new editions of this work were competing for the market in 1730 (published respectively by Roguet, van der Kloot and Libraires d'Amsterdam), and whoever secured the contract for two or three further volumes would be assured of an excellent business deal. The Compagnie des Libraires d'Amsterdam, which had just brought out its own reprint in August 1730, won the contract. This involved at least three further instalments, since volumes V, VI and VII appeared simultaneously in May 1731: the *Gazette d'Amsterdam* announced their publication on 22 May. Prévost took three or four months at most to write these, from January to mid-April; and *Manon Lescaut* seems to have cost him less than two month's work, around March and April. Volume V, devoted to his stay in England, was clearly written at speed, and volume VI completed the sequence of adventures of the Man of Quality. We must simply assume that Prévost subsequently devoted a little more time to perfecting the short novella which was to secure his fame. The care with which he set it apart – by means of a preface and preamble – from the stories and anecdotes assembled in volume VI of the *Mémoires et aventures* indicates the importance he attached to the short narrative which epitomized his art as a storyteller in 1731.

Nine years later, in one of the stories written for *Pour et Contre*, Prévost was to evoke briefly the climate in which he had composed *Manon Lescaut*, 'in a hostelry on the Ness': '. . . the sad situation of Amsterdam being in no way compensated for by the beauty of her canals and buildings, nothing can induce a man to retire there except in order to hide from the world, and make for himself a kind of sepulchre'. The anecdote in *Pour et Contre* about the life of foreigners in Amsterdam, which Prévost relates to this period of his life, recalls the atmosphere of mourning and mystery which at that time permeated his imagination. This is the 'sepulchre' (a highly Prévostian expression) or retreat to which we owe volume VII of the *Mémoires d'un homme de qualité*, subtitled: *Histoire du chevalier des Grieux et de Manon Lescaut*.

From Cleveland to Manon

In 1731, Antoine-François Prévost d'Exiles was thirty-four years old and still at the beginning of his career. Since joining the Benedictines in 1720 he had found in literature a source of distraction; in 1722 he had written *Les Aventures de Pomponius*, a short libertine novel about the Regency, and probably began writing the *Mémoires d'un homme de qualité*. In 1728 he had caused a scandal by fleeing to England, and in the same year achieved a great *succès d'émotion* with the first volume of the *Mémoires d'un homme de qualité*. In 1730 he embarked on *Le Philosophe anglais, ou Histoire de Monsieur Cleveland*, a long epic novel in which he attempted to express the essence of his dreams and his vision of the world. The hero, a bastard son of Cromwell, tries to shake off this curse by hiding away in the Devonshire caves, then by travelling through the New World, tireless in pursuit of Happiness and Truth. Then, at the point where Prévost decided to wind up the novel, he leads his hero into the midst of Appalachian savages and makes him suffer appalling catastrophes: his army has been decimated, his daughter abducted by cannibals and his wife is about to die in the wilds of Louisiana. Prévost was attempting to paint on a huge canvas what he described in the *Mémoires et aventures* as the 'extremes of evil'.

It seems clear that he interrupted this huge narrative in order to condense into a very classical novella the 'mass of unhappy life' which lay at the heart of Cleveland's story: in a few pages of *Manon Lescaut* he was to evoke the dream of happiness, the betrayal, the flight into the desert and the death of the loved one, whereas he will reserve several future volumes for Cleveland's religious and intellectual quest. Far from thinking of the *Histoire du chevalier des Grieux* as a kind of miracle in the novelistic career of Prévost, we should see it as the outcome of a long inquiry into the impossibility of happiness, the pervasiveness of evil and the misfortune attaching to the passions. The *Mémoires d'un homme de qualité* already focused on the death of the loved one and on a mourning that was without end; it already depicted half-mad lovers, fleeing their persecutors through the (new) world. In volume VI, the story of the misfortunes of John Law – the famous adventurer and financier of the Regent – foreshadows accurately enough the misfortunes of des Grieux. The great interrupted novel, *Cleveland*, also gives prominence to the misfortunes of love, to bereavement and to wanderings in the desert. If we consider Prévost's fiction as a whole, in other words the dozen novels written between 1722 and 1760, on either side of the unparalleled achievement of *Manon Lescaut*, it becomes clear that the themes of betrayed love, impossible happiness and mourning without end are the kernel of the Prévostian novel. What makes the story of des Grieux exceptional is its density, its tragic intensity together with a degree of verisimilitude to which Prévost had never before aspired.

Introduction

From Novel to Novella

The distinction between the 'novel' and the 'novella' dates from the period of French classicism: the 'novel' refers to a poetic form, close to epic, in which descriptions, portraits, psychological developments, sudden transformations – everything, in fact, that we may call 'ornament' – occupy a central place; the 'novella' is a short narrative, based around a dramatic plot, which preserves a close relation to historical or social reality. Sometimes the 'novella' enters the domain of the long novel in the guise of a detached story: a character can rapidly narrate the history of his misfortunes, often centring upon misunderstood or betrayed love. This device is found in the novels of La Calprenède or Mme de Scudéry, Prévost's favourite authors.

In his two full-length novels, *Mémoires et aventures* and *Cleveland*, Prévost constantly resorted to the convention of the detached story. But the writer who gave to this type of story its autonomy and its conventions is Robert Challe, author of the *Illustres Françaises* (1713). In this sequence of novellas with suggestive titles – *Histoire de Monsieur Des Prez et de Mademoiselle de l'Espine, Histoire de Monsieur Des Frans et de Sylvie* and so on – we can clearly trace the dual aesthetic of *Manon Lescaut*, whose combination of tragic grandeur and social realism can still astonish us today. Prévost had discovered in England (in Dryden's *All for Love* and in Lillo's *The London Merchant*) a new tragic formula, more brutal and more direct than Racinian tragedy; he had also encountered in the novels of Defoe and in the English press an unprecedented social realism. And later on he seems to have responded equally to Hogarth's satirical sequences, *The Harlot's Progress* and *The Rake's Progress*. All of this constituted for Prévost *'le gout anglais'*, to which from 1733 he was to devote part of his literary journal, *Pour et Contre*. But this taste, which seemed to him untranslatable or largely incompatible with French taste, required that he find a literary equivalent in French culture, and for him this equivalent was undoubtedly *Les Illustres Françaises*. It is difficult today to comprehend the profoundly scandalous nature of the tale narrated by Prévost in *Manon Lescaut*, 'this novel whose hero is a rogue and whose heroine a trollop who is led off to the Salpêtrière' (Montesquieu, in *Mes Pensées*). The shocking aspect of a novel which bordered on the libertine – in which a defrocked priest falls in love with a mercenary courtesan, agrees for her sake to cheat at cards, to murder and then flee to America – required an elegant, haughty and melancholic narrative to render it acceptable. Prévost's project seems to have been to pass off a social realism of the most brutal kind by virtue of an immaculate style.

Manon in the Age of Louis XIV

As is necessary in a novella, Prévost creates a very precise historical setting. It has long been thought that this referred to the Regency and to Paris in the period of Law's System (1715–22) – the world of pleasure, money and corruption which Prévost knew so well in his youth. But this is by no means the case, and the text informs us explicitly that the action takes place before the death of Louis XIV. The narrator (Monsieur de Renoncour, hero of the *Mémoires d'un homme de qualité*) offers us in the first line of the narrative proper a clearly restrictive chronological reference: 'I must take you back to the time when I first met the Chevalier des Grieux. It was about six months before I left for Spain.' Now Renoncour's voyage to Spain coincided exactly with the death of Louis XIV in the novel, which would have been familiar to contemporary readers, volume III having appeared in 1729. The departure of the protagonists to America therefore takes place at the very beginning of 1715, and their life in Paris, which lasts two and a half years, unfolds in its entirety between 1712 and 1715. The Regency has no place whatsoever in the action of *Manon Lescaut*, whose world is not that of speculation and paper money but of counting out one's louis d'or, of calculating fortunes according to an entirely traditional hierarchy of value, and of making money by the age-old means of prostitution and theft. The only dateable episode, that which takes place in the Hôtel de Transylvanie – at the time when the Prince of R. . . was living at Clagny – refers to the year 1714.

It is worth noting that had Prévost set his story during the Regency, its theme of general corruption would basically have been a commonplace; set in the reign of Louis XIV it becomes frankly subversive. Prévost describes a stable and hierarchical society, fundamentally moral and Christian, overtly hypocritical, in which the behaviour of the Chevalier must appear all the more scandalous. The inner torment of the Chevalier is correspondingly deeper: raised by Jesuits, respectful of religion and the social order, desirous to be reconciled with the authorities and to retain the friendship of Tiberge, there is nothing of the cynic or rebel about him. He dreams of a 'wise and ordered life', of a single and life-long passion consecrated by marriage. In no way does he resemble the characters of Crébillon. Manon herself is equally unfamiliar with Crébillonesque 'aberrations of the heart'; she makes a clear distinction between her pleasures or amusements and what is for her simply a resource or means of existence. As in the majority of his novels, Prévost brings adventurers, rebels and marginal characters into conflict with a traditional society. But he also conjures up a world that is disappearing, already in disintegration beneath a respectable façade. Thus the King has handed over power to commoner financiers; the Prince de Transylvanie retires to a monastery, yet lives off the proceeds of a gambling house; dukes and marquesses equally live by trickery. The nobility, like the Chevalier's father or the Lieutenant of Police, and the wealthy, like old M. de G. M., conspire in the end to preserve the semblances of moral order and deport Manon. In New Orleans society will behave similarly: the almoner and the governor conspire to prevent the lovers from marrying. But the old hierarchical, absolutist and Catholic world of Louis XIV is on the point of foundering; soon the dream of individual happiness and freedom will be able to express itself openly.

The Law of Money

The social order is constantly underlined, and the importance of money in this short novel is without analogy in eighteenth-century fiction. Money (or its absence) makes social distinctions visible at every turn; the ladder of income ruthlessly establishes these impassable frontiers. At the bottom there are the servants, who live on more or less nothing (less than 100 francs per year, probably, which is roughly equivalent to £1000 today). Even with their meagre incomes, des Grieux and Manon can each afford their servant. Coachmen argue over a franc, Marcel is bought for a louis d'or (24 francs), to him an enormous sum. One level above this there is Manon, whose parents send her to the convent with 300 francs. This is very little: in *La Religieuse*, Diderot's nun, who comes of good family, will speak of 3000 francs for a convent dowry. Manon, who knows the value of money, understands instantly that her 300 francs added to the 50 écus (150 francs) of her lover will not take them very far. To live modestly but comfortably, a single person like Tiberge needs an allowance of 3000 francs a year: that is what constitutes a bourgeois income in this novel. Des Grieux and Manon, enriched by the spoils extracted from M. de B., calculate that the 'respectable but simple' income necessary for them is 6000 francs per year. But given that they anticipate spending three-quarters of this on coaches, theatres and gambling, their budget turns out to be rather less than 'simple'. Between these expenses allowed as reasonable and those of the seriously rich people with whom the lovers consort, the gap is immense. M. de B. gives Manon 30,000 francs spending money per year, which would correspond to one-tenth of his income if we confine our calculation to the average revenues of a Farmer General of the time. Old M. de G. M. offers her nearly 10,000 francs in the first days of their acquaintance; as for his son, the young G. M. spends 40,000 francs a year on amusements and offers half of this to Manon. With such an income she can afford a liveried carriage, horses and servants, the prestige of which dazzles both herself and des Grieux.

That detail about the carriage is clearly significant: Manon dreams of one from the first; des Grieux does his utmost to procure one for her even if it means his ruin; it is to avoid the selling off of her '*équipage*' that, on the advice of her brother,

Manon sells herself to old M. de G. M.; and it is by means of a carriage that the young G. M. will make his conquest. The carriage is the symbol of a wealth which does not deceive. It defines a level of fortune that the lovers will never attain, and which they can at the very most usurp. For a carriage Manon steals the colossal sum of 60,000 francs from M. de B. Stripped of everything she will ultimately be brought to Le Havre in a heavy wagon, and she will end her short life exhausted by the walk through the desert. Never had the inevitability of society's laws been traced so remorselessly in a novel.

Social Distance

The impassable frontier between social classes also separates the lovers, and this is one of the most original aspects of the *Histoire du chevalier*. The social status of the Chevalier is easy to define: the younger son of an old noble family, he must consent to his elder brother receiving the majority of the future inheritance. He himself is destined for the Church, as is the custom, but will receive his 'rightful' share of the maternal and paternal inheritance – very much larger certainly than Tiberge's allowance – and it is this sum which he is impatiently awaiting. Manon on the other hand will never have more than the 300 francs with which she starts out. That Prévost in the 1731 edition should have described her as 'of sufficiently good birth' was a concession to the fictional conventions of the day; in a 1753 variant he was to describe her as 'of common stock', and this is far more plausible: her arrival unaccompanied at Amiens, her mediocre dowry, her complicity with a gangsterish brother, her mercenary habits and the absence of family intervention at the moment of her deportation are sufficient proof of her very low bourgeois background. Only her education would allow us to claim that she is not a daughter of the common people. Between the younger son of the nobility and this girl of obscure origins any lasting relationship or, to a certain extent, any deep understanding, is impossible. Des Grieux will refuse to accept that she is mercenary, that she lets herself be dazzled too easily, that she is afraid of going hungry, and that she lives for pleasure and in the present. All this shocks him. Manon in turn does not understand his anger, nor that he loves her despite events: when he follows her to America and proposes to marry her, she is overwhelmed. Thus each is to the other a living enigma.

On the other hand, we sense very strongly in the course of the narrative the complicity of class which unites the rich, and that which unites the poor. As early as the preamble at Pacy, the narrator Renoncour recognizes in des Grieux an equal, 'a man of birth and upbringing', whereas he finds Manon 'inscrutable', at once whore and princess. Later on, we see the same spontaneous complicity unite des Grieux and the young M. de T., and unite even the Lieutenant of Police and the young G. M. On the other hand Manon, whom all men are destined to find '*fatale*' or 'inscrutable', is instantly understood by the first witness in the narrative who speaks on her behalf, 'the old woman who emerged from the inn wringing her hands and shouting that it was a wicked shame and enough to give anyone the horrors'. For this old woman has guessed in her own way part of the drama that follows; she has in the course of her life seen other girls of poor background fall into prostitution and end as badly as Manon; she knows the 'wicked shame' which can befall women. As a woman of the people, she reacts spontaneously with a gesture and a cry.

But this cry in some sense describes a trivial event, the real nature of which none of the characters, and especially not the men, could suspect. The scene in Pacy is the overture to what is in reality a social tragedy, intended to inspire – as high tragedy does – 'fear' and 'pity'. More than once in *Manon Lescaut*, unassuming witnesses, speaking from another world to that of the narrator, allow us to understand that this almost banal story can be judged differently. The Saint-Denis innkeeper is moved to pity for the youth of the lovers and the strength of their passion; the attendant in the Salpêtrière Hospital is softened by Manon's 'angelic sweetness' and does everything in his power to release her; the Châtelet concierge also shows himself full of compassion for des Grieux; and Marcel, des Grieux's last servant, accompanies him as far as he can in his misfortune. Clearly it is in the common people that there is to be found sympathy for youth, indulgence to lovers, horror at police repression. It is also the case that the Chevalier always knows where to find favourable witnesses in his defence, however unassuming these may be.

The Personal Narrative

The distinguishing characteristic of the *Histoire* is that it is narrated by the Chevalier. We may imagine the same story as told respectively by Manon, Tiberge, the Lieutenant of Police, the Chevalier's father, the convent Superior, M. de T., Marcel, or by the novelist himself. But it would not be the same story. The other witnesses would all after their fashion command an objective voice; that of the Chevalier is not objective. Of everyone involved, it is he who must give us the most ambiguous version of events. Prévost carefully cultivated this aspect of his narrative. It will be noted that on the last page of the novella, after Manon's death, Tiberge, who had followed the lovers as far as Le Havre, rejoins the Chevalier in New Orleans a year and a half later, having been taken prisoner by 'Spanish corsairs'. This delay, which Prévost explains in a fairly cavalier manner, is of signal importance in the framing of the story. For the novelist, it is essential that Tiberge should not catch up with the lovers in New Orleans: his good sense would have averted the tragedy; he would have understood immediately that Synnelet was not ill-intentioned and that the desert was dangerous; he would have spoiled the wonderful movement of panic which seizes the lovers at the end.

But it is also essential that Tiberge should not be the sole confidant of the Chevalier. Despite owing him so much, it is not to Tiberge that des Grieux addresses his long confession, but to two strangers encountered in Calais. Renoncour and his pupil Rosemont, heroes of the *Mémoires et aventures*, are naturally more indulgent listeners, since they too have experienced misfortune in love. The account destined for ears such as these invites compassion rather than moral judgement. And it is also essential that des Grieux should have to wait nine months after Manon's death before being able to tell his story. These nine months are accumulated in the last pages of the novel, with a meticulous care on the part of the novelist: too soon after Manon's death the hero would have been shattered, exhausted, rebellious, incapable of standing back from events; too long after his return to France and he would have acquired wisdom and been able to distance himself from this youthful adventure. He would by then have assimilated its sense and significance. Nine months after her death, he is half-way between despair and recollection in tranquillity, between passion and wisdom; he can describe his experiences with emotion, yet present his vindication coherently and 'with the most natural ease of manner'. The tuning of narrative distance between the tale and its telling also determines the style. For it is this mixture of sadness and discreet humour, lyricism and disenchantment, passion and sweet reasonableness, that produces the overall tone of melancholy so peculiar to the Chevalier's recitative.

The Indirect Narrative

The personal narrative was certainly not a novelty in 1731, and Robert Challe had in *Les Illustres Françaises* given Prévost a range of registers which he had only to exploit. Memoirs written in the first person had enjoyed a considerable vogue around 1700. But the classical memoir writers were oblivious to the temporalities of the memoir as such: the events described were laid down flat, as in an historical account. In des Grieux's narrative, we continually sense a gap between the actual time of the narration and the distancing of past events, a difference between the narrator as he was formerly and as he is in the present tense of the story. This gap varies: the Chevalier can soften when he recalls the meeting of the young lovers and mock himself for his own naïvety. Later on, he experiences a certain embarrassment in describing his cunning, the concessions made to Manon's brother, the flagrant breaches of honour. In the second part, the incomprehension between the lovers increases, the tone is more impatient and dramatic and the more recent past seems to come back to life in scenes of extremely precise dialogue.

This unstable relation between the relived past and an anxious, traumatized memory makes the Chevalier's narrative astonishingly mobile and alive. Everything that was said, everything that happened, is filtered through memory and made present by an unremittingly partial and impassioned narrator. This is particularly noticeable in the treatment of speech. The narrative consists of one long soliloquy, which in real time would last more than four hours. Nobody other than the Chevalier has the floor, and every voice reaches us through his mediation. It is the longest exercise in indirect speech to have appeared in a fictional narrative up to this period. But the operation of memory means that the words of the other characters, particularly of Manon, are made present to us, often more vividly than direct speech in the theatre. In more than one passage we could translate the indirect speech into direct speech, an exercise which would show that what is most original in Prévost's art would be lost in such translation. Thus the first meeting between des Grieux and Manon, consisting of the commonplaces allowable when one is striking up a conversation: 'I asked her what brought her to Amiens and whether she knew anybody there. She answered quite simply that she had been sent there by her parents to become a nun.' This report conjures up the 'ingenuousness' and simplicity of Manon, but also her sadness, her total absence of vocation, her apparent resignation – where direct speech would merely have given us information. Similarly in the second, decisive sentence that she speaks (for in this semblance of dialogue which the Chevalier passes on to us, Manon has so far uttered only one sentence): 'She remained silent for some time and then said that she knew quite well that she was going to be miserable, but that she supposed it must be God's will, since He had not shown her any other way out.' The Chevalier's narrative preserves intact the moment that is going to change his fate: that moment when Manon remains silent to ponder a little stratagem (each of Manon's silences in the story invites us to question her motives); she adopts a pathetic expression, almost pained, before resorting to the only way out that heaven has in fact shown her: the Chevalier himself, who is powerless to resist 'her air of wistful sadness' or 'the soft appeal of her eyes'.

Generally speaking, des Grieux's narrative privileges speech reported from the distant past, and he preserves its intonations intact. Indirect speech takes on all the nuances of living conversation, but with an effect of distance which renders it more moving, and sometimes slightly old-fashioned (as in the case of old G. M.), or amusing, as in this sentence which offers a glimpse of the farcical and mischievous character of Manon's brother: 'He impudently admitted that he had always thought the same way himself, but that once his sister had broken the laws of her sex – *albeit with the man he liked best in the world* – he had only made his peace with her in the hope of making a bit out of her misconduct.' In the Chevalier's sentence we seem to hear a sudden echo of Lescaut's truculent manner. Towards the characters in his drama des Grieux behaves as an artist: each one appears before us and is fixed in the memory by a turn of phrase, an opinion, a gesture: thus the Father Superior of Saint-Lazare, indulgent and slightly senile, or old G. M. with his old-world attentions and compliments, or the Lieutenant of Police with his exquisite courtesy.

Des Grieux as Artist

The Chevalier des Grieux is in many respects a master storyteller. He endeavours to win over two interlocutors who have helped him in a moment of great anguish: he thanks them by relating a fine story in which he will prove his nobility of soul, his aristocratic taste and his purity of motive. He will not give in to despair or protestation; he structures the drama of his misfortunes with a skill which allows him to reserve for later, after supper, 'something still more interesting in the sequel to his story' (end of Part One). This disinterested confession aims nevertheless to move and convince listeners or readers as to his good faith: 'You will no doubt blame my behaviour but I am sure you will not be able to help pitying me.' In fact, this plea for the defence *pro domo* employs all the devices of the most elaborate rhetoric.

Inspection reveals that not once but seven times in his story does des Grieux attempt to convince, move and win over a variety of interlocutors, using methods that are the same in each case. He pleads his cause, in summary fashion, to Lescaut, describing his 'mishaps' and his 'fears'; he develops the theme with considerable virtuosity before Tiberge: 'I talked about my passion with all the vehemence it inspired in me [. . .] I represented it as one of those peculiar blows, against which virtue is defenceless and wisdom cannot be forearmed, which Destiny aims at some poor wretch when she is bent on his destruction'; with the Father Superior of Saint-Lazare he takes up the narrative of his 'long and unconquerable passion' with enough affliction in his voice to completely convert the good monk. However it is the Lieutenant of Police, M. de T., his own father and the Governor of New Orleans who in turn constitute the real jury whom the Chevalier must win over. Here his methods, though adapted to each circumstance, remain despite everything the same: as in Ciceronian rhetoric, which he assimilated so thoroughly at College in Amiens, des Grieux must include, within a formal apology, an introduction, an appeal to the auditor's clemency (*captatio benevolentiae*), a recourse to *pathos* (to speak passionately about passion, despairingly about despair), a dramatized narrative complete with ornaments (irreparable calamities, sudden reversals, the fickleness of Fortune) and finally, a well-paced peroration. He employs all these devices with consummate skill, certain of winning his case. He similarly employs them with Renoncour, in other words with the reader; and his intention is to work into his defence as many revolting admissions as possible, without losing face and without ceasing to appear the victim of fate. We are thus caught in the nets of an insidious argumentation, entirely deliberate but concealed at every point behind the emotions of the moment and by that sublime melancholy which characterizes permanent grief. Des Grieux is no longer a rebel or a hopeless case, but an artist in control of himself and already a writer. This vocation is apparent very early on: from his first separation from Manon, following the episode in the Rue Vivienne, he devotes more than a year to his sorrows, to reflection and to literature: 'I wrote a sentimental commentary on the fourth book of the *Aeneid*; I still hope to publish it and venture to think the public will find it interesting.' The taste for literary fame and the sense of a public are not the food of a desperate man or a suicide. The Chevalier's future, after the final separation and the renunciation of his errors, is sketched out in advance. He will become a writer; he will create the 'sentimental commentary' on his own adventures. Besides, in the last line of his narrative there is no longer any question of returning to Saint-Sulpice or embarking for Malta. There is no mention even of his interlocutors: Renoncour, who in the other volumes of the *Mémoires et aventures* was accustomed to reappear and comment upon the doings of his chance companions and draw their moral, is silent – des Grieux has transformed him into the secretary of his own story.

The Looped Narrative

This is surely the inherent problem with all personal narratives: whoever the hero-narrator in question, the novelist always has to show him turning slowly into the gifted author of his own story. A personal narrative always catches up with itself at the point where the hero decides to take up the pen and record what has taken place . . . This is the case with Gil Blas, a picaresque hero with no obvious literary inclinations; it is the case with the heroine of *La Vie de Mariane*, an obscure seamstress who at the start of the novel might surprise us by being able to write as well as Marivaux, though the work as a whole persuades us of this. And it is likewise the case with des Grieux, though we know from the very outset that he was a model student at college who, when restored to his senses, dreams of writing in solitude. What remains astonishing in his case is that this moralist versed in Virgil, St Augustine and Malebranche, capable of fashioning his lover's vows with 'a profane mixture of amorous and theological language', should show so little of the moralist in his narrative. The only authorities which guide his pen are those which guided his life while with Manon: Venus and the Goddess Fortuna. And yet this defence of love is shaped by the hand of a master. By comparison with other personal narratives of the eighteenth century (by Lesage, Hamilton, Challe, Marivaux, Crébillon and others), the *Histoire du chevalier des Grieux* eschews any kind of improvisation, disorder or affected negligence. Prévost, who had broken new ground in the *Mémoires et aventures* by multiplying narrative digressions, reflections and meditations, seems with *Manon Lescaut* to have made a point of writing the simplest and most structured of his works.

At first we are reminded of the unities of classical tragedy: *Manon* strikes us as a kind of narrative in five acts, fraught with bleakness and grandeur. But the development is not that of a tragedy. It is founded less on an ineluctable progression than on the principle of repetition: three times Manon betrays the Chevalier; three times he forgives her; three times they are punished – and in an increasingly dramatic pattern. In this sense the plot of *Manon* resembles a Molière comedy; one thinks of *L'Ecole des femmes* or *Le Misanthrope*. In these examples a psychological conflict deepens in the course of three trials, each of the same type. The art lies entirely in avoiding repetition while insisting upon the repetition of situation, since neither Arnolphe, Alceste nor des Grieux ever learn their lessons, and experience is wasted on them. In the *Histoire du chevalier des Grieux* we have to marvel at the way Prévost succeeds in treating differently, on three occasions, fundamentally identical situations: the financial ruin of the lovers, Manon's fright, her spontaneous betrayal, the Chevalier's despair, their impossible attempts at understanding and their inevitable reconciliations.

The invention with which Prévost handles this looped structure is unique. And judging from the details he includes it is clear that he sought to multiply within the story internal echoes and what might be termed narrative rhymes. The opening scene at Pacy is one example. The narrator, Renoncour, has been held up by a crowd; two heavy wagons have just arrived at an inn and people gather round, impelled by a vague curiosity. An old woman emerges from the inn and prompts the Man of Quality to enter. He forces himself through and manages to catch sight of Manon, chained among a group of prostitutes, Manon who is trying to avoid being looked at and hides her face. If we keep in mind this meticulous structure with its gradual focusing, we see that it precisely anticipates the scene of the lovers' first meeting in Amiens, described a few pages further on. There also, we are in the courtyard of an inn where a coach has just arrived, though now the circle of women breaks up immediately, the inn-yard is empty, and Manon remains alone and offered up to view. The scenes in Pacy and in Amiens are thus to be read in counterpoint: the latter concludes and the former inaugurates Manon's brief voyage through life. Similarly, des Grieux in the courtyard at Amiens accedes to life: he confidently walks forward towards Manon, he finds the words with which to address her, and he embarks on a sentimental education. Here is a kind of birth; at Pacy on the other hand, he is discovered sitting in a corner of the inn, 'apparently unconscious of everything around him', an image of death. I have pointed out in passing other narrative rhymes of this kind: the rapid journey of the lovers from Amiens to Paris finds an echo in the slow march of the convoy which brings them from Paris to Pacy; Manon's passion for coaches leads to the long trek from which she dies. The image of the wheel of fortune, the cycle of misfortune, and the looped narrative are what create the profound unity of this work.

Free Will or Determinism

The characteristic domain of fiction is to depict the course of existence, to provoke an interrogation of the meaning of life. This is particularly true of eighteenth-century fiction, whether in the works of Voltaire or Diderot, Fielding or Goethe. Prévost is however the first to make of the novel (from the *Mémoires et aventures* and *Cleveland* onwards) a meditation on human destiny. And even des Grieux's apology contains this questioning aspect: he tries to explain away the faults and crimes with which he has rightly been charged, making fate or God himself responsible. And when he calls himself the victim of fate, led by 'the ascendant of his destiny' or by the caprices of Fortune, we are doubtless tempted to regard such justifications as facile. Similarly when he confronts Tiberge, the disciple of Saint-Sulpice and of the Jesuits, with the Jansenist argument: 'Do I have any power over my actions?' we understand him to be claiming that he has been the victim of a force stronger than his will, a 'charm' or 'spell' which by the end of his story is slowly wearing off.

Naturally, these are arguments which allow him to shirk all responsibility. But they seem none the less to lie at the root of Prévost's psychology. It is quite true that des Grieux has wanted to forget Manon, that he has prayed, read Saint Augustine, and chosen with real pleasure the path of study and wisdom. But a greater and more tangible pleasure – the sight of Manon – throws him back into confusion. According to what was called at the time the theory of 'the two delights', all of our desires are structured thus: 'one passion gives birth to them, another passion can as easily destroy them'. Without supernatural aid, how can we triumph over the siren promptings of nature, which are by definition irresistible? This sums up what might be called Prévost's Jansenism in 1731. At the end of the novel, he even seems to fall into a kind of Jansenist radicalism: at the moment when the Chevalier and his mistress return to the path of duty and prepare themselves for marriage Heaven decides to oppose them, in the person of the New Orleans almoner. And the final punishment comes from a Hidden God, in a silent and absurdist universe. Between the life lived according to nature and the life of complete renunciation there is no middle road.

It can be argued that this is the vision of the hero, not of the author. The latter expresses himself through the work as a whole, and in a markedly ambiguous manner. Thus the Preface draws a wholly traditional Christian moral from the story, in which we see the free will of the hero affirmed: 'I have to portray a young man who obstinately refuses to be happy and deliberately plunges into the most dire misfortunes; who, though gifted with all the qualities which go to make up the most brilliant merit, chooses an obscure and vagabond life ...' And this is also what des Grieux himself seems to maintain at the end, when he describes himself as returned to his senses. Yet the entire narrative has shown the contrary: des Grieux thought he had found happiness but instead found himself drawn powerlessly into a cycle of misfortune and deceit. Once returned to his senses, he does not in the least repudiate the happiness he has glimpsed, and will pass the rest of his life in mourning Manon. She is the only meaning, the only source of value that he has discovered in his own life. If he has freedom, it is in the choice that he makes to live for Manon, and to extol her for the rest of his days. At the very most he will acknowledge that such happiness is an image of the happiness of the saints above – and that too could be said by a Jansenist. What des Grieux cannot do is ignore or spurn the call of nature. This is undoubtedly Prévost's guiding idea, already at the time of writing *Manon Lescaut* and increasingly so in his career thereafter: nature is good and makes pleasure our guide, from which nobody can shield himself. The call of nature can be observed more clearly in the young, like Manon, and in the common people; but the varnish of education which the privileged may allow themselves will not resist the force of the passions, which are in all cases both irresistible and fundamentally good. This is the conclusion at which Prévost arrives again and again: the passions are good in themselves, only the value of their object allows us to call them morally good or evil. And this is why des Grieux would have been a true hero had he met Didon rather than Manon. The bad move, the fatal object-choice, was Manon. And if Manon ends by seeming so seductive a figure, that is the ruse of the devil – or of literature. From such a perspective there remains little room for free will. From Jansenist pessimism, which insists on the weight of original sin and the insuperable misery of man, Prévost has slipped into a deterministic sensualism, increasingly evident in his writings, but whose earliest expression is *Manon Lescaut*.

The Metaphysics of Sentiment

Like all Prévost's works from this period, the *Histoire du chevalier des Grieux* is impregnated with metaphysical preoccupations. The essential problems are not whether des Grieux could have been happy in his studies at Amiens or Saint-Sulpice, nor whether Manon is punished excessively for her fickleness, but whether their happiness was condemned by God from the outset, and if love is itself a sin. Moreover, Prévost's psychology is not aimed at describing the varieties of humankind, but at subjecting his characters to ordeals which reveal their fundamental desires and bring them up against the unknowable. A few rapid strokes suffice Prévost to characterize Manon, or Lescaut, or Tiberge, or the Chevalier's father; on this point he easily contents himself with the stereotypes of traditional comedy, from Plautus to Dancourt. And what really do we know about des Grieux, peculiar to himself? A good student, a good seminarian, a good friend, a good son, a good lover, he has never chased after originality; only his passion for Manon distinguishes him from what he calls 'the common run of men'. But the passion of love rends him and lays bare all the hidden forces of his sensibility, revealing an unlimited capacity for pleasure and pain.

The intensity of this passion in fact overwhelms his entire being and brings in train an infinite number of unexpected reactions and contradictory emotions. This is what he explains to Renoncour to redeem the shame of his incarceration in Saint-Lazare: 'Most men are touched only by five or six passions, and their whole life, with all its storms and stresses, moves round within this circle. Take away love and hatred, pleasure and sorrow, hope and fear, and there is nothing else they feel. But characters of a more delicate texture can be tossed about in a hundred different ways; they seem to have more than five senses, and to be a prey of ideas and sensations surpassing the ordinary limits of nature.' An exceptional passion, affecting a sensitive and sincere individual, multiplies his 'secondary' passions. Using the language of a young aristocrat, des Grieux is led to believe that nobility of birth and nobility of soul are one and the same; but in the course of the narrative we come to understand that the intensity of the passion alone creates the inner landscape of the lover: his happiness, anxieties, anger, heartache, hope, melancholy, humiliations, pride, remorse. What makes the character of des Grieux unique – of which he is moreover so proud – is the intensity of his passion, and this violence generates all kinds of irrational behaviour, in joy as much as in despair. It is difficult today for us to appreciate the exceptional nature of these 'movements of the heart', and yet they are perceived by the Chevalier's circle as unique of their kind. When des Grieux learns for the first time that Manon has betrayed him, he takes four steps and collapses as if struck by lightning. When all their money is stolen at Chaillot, he falls into 'a tortured state' and thinks of killing himself. When, in Saint-Lazare, M. de G. M. informs him that Manon is imprisoned in the Hôpital Général, he falls into 'an uncontrollable rage' and tries to strangle the old man: 'You cannot imagine how I shouted and wept in my anguish, and my behaviour was so frenzied that the others, not knowing the reason, looked at each other with as much alarm as amazement.'

These spectacular explosions are, at the beginning of the novel, the acts of a very young man; later on, after a new betrayal by Manon, we shall see him fall into 'a sullen and gloomy calm', followed by a 'terrible outburst of rage'. When Manon dies, he relates that 'no tear fell from my eyes nor did any sigh escape my lips': his internalized despair leading him to a kind of suicide by the will, a death from grief – that condition for which the English coined the phrase 'a broken heart'. In excesses of grief, as in excesses of joy, the soul can split up and destroy itself.

Such is Prévost's psychology, which comes close to

metaphysics, since it concerns itself always with states which take the individual to their limit, up against the borders of the knowable. Through these extremes of behaviour, des Grieux interrogates both nature and God: was man created to inhabit unliveable states of being? Does love drive him into the negation of what he is? Do the longings of his heart lead him into excesses from which there is no exit? Following the Chevalier's narrative we retain the impression that the most generous aspirations and expansions of the heart are doomed to failure, at the hands both of society which represses them and a God who punishes them. Prévost is not interested in individual cases nor does he aspire to psychological realism. He is preoccupied with man's destiny, and the impossibility of all dialogue with an ambivalent nature and an inscrutable God. Prévost's investigation belongs with what contemporaries termed the '*métaphysique du coeur*', a philosophical trend which is encountered particularly in the words of Mme de Lambert, Fénelon, Mme de Guyon and Malebranche.

An Aesthetics of Contrast

Such is the paradox of the *Histoire du chevalier des Grieux et de Manon Lescaut*. The anecdotal basis of the story is simple, almost banal, almost like a newspaper item. As with many short novels of the time published anonymously in Holland, it contains a defrocked priest, a young woman of easy virtue, a rather naïve young gentleman deceived by a coquette, some ridiculous financiers, escapades, duels, escapes, and even a voyage to America. Prévost gave his booksellers all the ingredients of a bestseller. But he gives a tragic development to this libertine tale, establishes its proportions with great care, and chooses a style of severe purity, with invocations to Horace and Virgil. Resolved on a career as a writer, under the name of 'Prévost d'Exiles' which he had just invented, he leaves clues everywhere as to his story's status as a literary work inspired by the best models.

Nor on the other hand can there be any doubt that the subject affects him deeply for personal reasons. It is no longer thought today that *Manon Lescaut* is autobiographical: to claim otherwise we would need to know the details of his private life between 1715 and 1730 – which is far from being the case. But what we can say is that the *Histoire du chevalier* is full of allusions to Prévost's own life. He too was educated by the Jesuits in a northern French town and taken under the wing of the bishop of Amiens. Like des Grieux he arrived in Paris in 1712–13, at a similar age, and entered a monastery after 'an unhappy affair' – the details of which he never revealed – subsequently fleeing the cloister for a life of adventure. But only this last episode created a scandal, and all the autobiographical clues we possess are known only from Prévost himself. He certainly did not intend to tell his life story in *Manon Lescaut*, but more than once he finds himself pointing up a kind of affinity between himself and his hero. What can be said positively is that des Grieux's intellectual preoccupations are in many respects his creator's: the hesitation between Jesuit and Jansenist positions, between a providential God and a hidden God, between confidence in the workings of nature and a radical pessimism, between free will and determinism. Similarly des Grieux's vain search for serenity and happiness, his feverish quest for pleasure and obsession with death all inform Prévost's fiction between 1728 and 1731.

These preoccupations run through the *Histoire du chevalier* in abbreviated and tormented form, giving an impression of absolute sincerity. Whereas *Cleveland* develops the same themes in a lengthy and moving meditation, the *Histoire du chevalier* gives them an allusive and fleeting aspect by varying the narrative tones and registers. We find humour, sentimental fancy, farce and the light atmosphere of a comedy of manners – as well as the starkest tragedy. The extraordinary success of this short novel undoubtedly derives from this aesthetic of contrast, with its economy of construction and mobility of narration.

The Fortunes of a Little Work

Prévost was clearly very conscious of his effects in *Manon Lescaut*.

He certainly did not throw down on paper a kind of spontaneous confession, in an overwhelming burst of sincerity, as was commonly thought in the Romantic period. In the authorial Preface which opens the work he set forth the most classical of precepts: 'I am well aware that a narrative must be lightened of circumstances that might make it cumbersome and involved.' The show of purism which is aired in this Preface reflects the tastes of 'the Man of Quality', but also Prévost's own taste. There is nothing improvised about des Grieux's narrative: it observes the rules of tact, propriety and *'bonne grâce'*. It is very clear that Prévost sought to reproduce the ease of faultless aristocratic speech: the style is manifestly that of 'a man who knows the world and also has delicacy of mind', as he will later characterize M. de T. Prévost submits to this model in the smallest details of his narrative. Moreover, when he came to re-read the book twenty years later, it was still to this stylistic decorum that he would pay the closest attention, as witness the eight hundred corrections incorporated into the 1753 edition. But it is also true that the welcome accorded the novel caused Prévost to consider it subsequently in a slightly different light.

The novel's success was not immediate, and at first nobody seemed to distinguish the *Histoire du chevalier* from the rest of the *Mémoires et aventures*. But the earliest reviews of any length already suggest the interest inspired by the character of Manon. La Barre de Beaumarchais wrote in *Lettres sérieuses et badines*, shortly after the appearance of the novel: 'There is something yet more striking about the betrothed girl. She appreciates virtue but adores pleasure, and this love of riches and amusements leads her to betray at every turn both virtue and Chevalier.' This moralizing and sentimental interpretation gained ground in the years that followed, culminating at the point when the work began to be widely available in France, towards the end of 1733. Effectively banned in this year, the novel suddenly became – as is very common in such cases – a huge success.

It was in 1733 that *Les Aventures du chevalier des Grieux et de Manon Lescaut* began to be reprinted separately (once in 1733, twice in 1734). And it was now that Prévost reprinted in *Pour et Contre* the opinion expressed in the *Lettres sérieuses et badines*, but exaggerating further its sentimental emphasis: des Grieux has by now become 'an unhappy slave of love', and Manon loves her Chevalier 'with desperate passion'. Having just returned to France, Prévost obviously preferred a *succès d'émotion* to a *succès de scandale*. And the success of *Manon Lescaut* (*Histoire de Manon Lescaut*, from 1756) was rapidly growing. Prévost was sufficiently aware of this to offer a thoroughly revised edition in 1753: 'It is to comply with the entreaties of those who are devoted to this little work that we have determined to purge it of a large number of vulgar errors which slipped into the early editions . . .' This new edition, on luxury paper with illustrations by Pasquier and Gravelot, amply attests to Prévost's partiality towards his 'little work'.

Nor is there any doubt as to the continued success of the novel throughout the century. Between 1731 and Prévost's death in 1763 we can count more than twenty editions of the *Mémoires et aventures* and eight editions of the *Histoire du chevalier des Grieux et de Manon Lescaut* – though it remained the case that up until 1823 the majority of readers continued to read *Manon Lescaut* as volume VII of the *Mémoires d'un homme de qualité*.

Concerning 'Masterpieces'

The fate of *Manon Lescaut* invites us to reflect upon the status of masterpieces. Prévost, who was very attuned to public taste, regarded this brief narrative, which cost him so little time, as the most moving and attractive of his works. He knew this from the outset, when he accorded it so important a position at the end of the *Mémoires et aventures*. His readers made it a success, but its pre-eminence was not established until after the author's death. Palissot wrote in the *Nécrologe*: 'Perhaps the masterpiece of his pen, despite the partiality he displayed towards *Cleveland*, was – and more than one man of taste will agree – the *Histoire du chevalier des Grieux et de Manon Lescaut*.' The author of the preface to the *Oeuvres choisies* of 1783 agreed: 'We doubt whether this work is not its author's masterpiece.' Faced with the extent of Prévost's fictional writings, readers hesitated to admit a preference for a small work of two hundred pages, and it was only with the Romantic period that *Manon Lescaut* took its place as an incomparable account of the workings of the human heart, a universal masterpiece. Extricated from the *Mémoires d'un homme de qualité*, it now shone with its own brilliance.

The popularity of *Manon Lescaut* has increased consistently ever since, at the expense of all Prévost's other fiction. Through the more than two hundred and fifty editions published between 1731 and 1981, the work's double nature has taken hold: a popular novel which is often reprinted in cheap editions, adapted for the theatre, opera and cinema; and at the same time a 'classic', a model of the fine writing promised by luxury editions and collections of 'Masterpieces of the French Novel' and enshrined in scholarly editions. As the scandalous and libertine dimension of the novel evaporated with the evolution of manners, *Manon Lescaut* has become a set text in schools and colleges, in the guise of innumerable paperback editions. Through its dual nature as a libertine and a serious work, at once popular and refined, and through its combination of social realism and classical rigour, it has successively reached every audience – men and women, old connoisseurs and young students, readers from all classes in all countries; it has achieved, by successive waves, universality. The variety of the registers on which Prévost touches has guaranteed him the widest possible audience.

This extraordinary consecration – *Manon Lescaut* remains after two centuries the most reprinted novel in French literature – should not blind us to a yet stranger mystery: the disrepute into which the rest of Prévost's huge fictional oeuvre, as human, as moving, and as masterly, has fallen, cast into the shadows by the triumphal success of *Manon Lescaut*. By interrupting *Cleveland*, his favourite work, in order to write in five or six weeks the *Histoire du chevalier*, Prévost was perhaps hoping to open the doors of his fictional universe to a much wider public and usher them into that 'moral world' so distinctively his; yet this was the only respect in which, to this day, he may be said to have failed.

Jean Sgard

BIBLIOGRAPHY

Editions:

Histoire du chevalier des Grieux et de Manon Lescaut, ed. Frédéric Deloffre and Raymond Picard, Paris, 'Classiques Garnier', 1965.

Oeuvres de Prévost, General Editor Jean Sgard, Presses Universitaires de Grenoble, 8 vols., 1976–86. The *Histoire du chevalier des Grieux et de Manon Lescaut* appears in vol. 1, and is annotated in vol. 8.

Histoire du chevalier des Grieux et de Manon Lescaut, ed. Jean Sgard, Paris, GF-Flammarion, 1995.

Studies:

Sgard, Jean, *Prévost romancier*, Paris, J. Corti, 1968, rev. ed. 1989.

Monty, Jeanne, 'Les Romans de l'abbé Prévost', in *Studies on Voltaire and the Eighteenth Century*, LXXVIII, Geneva, 1970.

Sgard, Jean, *L'Abbé Prévost, Labyrinthes de la mémoire*, Paris, Presses Universitaires de France, 1986.

Francis, R. A., *The Abbé Prévost's First-Person Narrators*, Oxford, The Voltaire Foundation, 1993.

TRANSLATOR'S NOTE

Prévost's novel was written in huge paragraphs and two long parts with no break. When I was preparing this translation of the text, it seemed a good idea to the then Editor of Penguin Classics and to me to break up these large slabs into shorter paragraphs and the parts into chapters. Also he encouraged my idea of short subject-headings to pages. I have left these features partly to simplify reprinting and partly as an act of piety in memory of Dr E. V. Rieu, most helpful of editors and the kindest of friends.

L.W.T.

MANON LESCAUT

PREFACE

By the Author of *The Memoirs of a Man of Quality*

I MIGHT have inserted the adventures of the Chevalier des Grieux into my Memoirs, but it seemed to me that, as there was no real connexion between them, the reader might find it more satisfactory to have them separated. The thread of my own story would have been cut for too long by a narrative of this size. I am far from being an exact writer, but I am well aware that a narrative must be lightened of circumstances that might make it cumbersome and involved. As Horace says:

> *Ut jam nunc dicat jam nunc debentia dici,*
> *Pleraque differat, ac praesens in tempus omittat.*[1]

Nor is such an eminent authority needed to demonstrate such a simple truth, for the prime source of this rule is common sense.

If the public has found some slight enjoyment and interest in the story of my life, I daresay it will be no less pleased with this addition. It will see in the conduct of M. des Grieux a terrible example of the strength of passion. I have to portray a young man who obstinately refuses to be happy and deliberately plunges into the most dire misfortunes; who, though gifted with all the qualities which go to make up the most brilliant merit, chooses an obscure and vagabond life in preference to all the advantages bestowed by nature and fortune; who foresees his misfortunes, but has not the will to avoid them; who is sensible of them and is overwhelmed by them, but cannot benefit by remedies constantly held out to him which might at any moment put an end to them; in fine, an ambiguous character, a mixture of virtues and vices, a perpetual contrast between good impulses and bad actions. Such is the substance of the picture I present. People of good sense will not regard a work of this nature as labour lost. Apart from the pleasure of interesting reading, they will find few things in it which may not serve as lessons in the art of living, and in my opinion it is no small service to the public to instruct while entertaining.

One cannot reflect upon the precepts of morality without being amazed to see them at one and the same time revered and neglected, and one wonders what is the explanation of this strange contradiction of the human heart that draws it towards theories of good and perfection which in practice it repels. If people of a certain order of intelligence and breeding will consider what is the most usual subject of their conversation or even of their private meditations, they will readily notice that they almost always turn upon some moral question. The most agreeable moments of their lives are those they spend, whether alone or with a friend, in examining with a candid mind the charms of virtue, the joys of friendship, the ways of attaining happiness, and frailties of human nature which deny us that happiness and remedies for these frailties. Horace and Boileau indicate this sort of conversation as one of the finest elements in their picture of the happy life. How then does it come about that we so easily fall from these lofty speculations and find ourselves so soon brought down to the level of the most commonplace of men? I am much mistaken if the reason I am going to adduce does not explain this contradiction between our theories and our behaviour. It is this: all moral precepts are so vague and generalized that it is very difficult to apply them directly to our specific manners and actions.

Let us take an example. Well-born souls feel that gentleness and humanity are virtues to be admired and are instinctively inclined to practise them; but once they are faced with action they often remain in doubt. Is this really the right moment? How far should one go? Is one not mistaken about the object in view? A hundred perplexities intervene. Even when wishing to be generous and charitable one is afraid of being a dupe; by seeming too tender-hearted and too easily moved one fears to appear weak; in a word, one is afraid of overdoing or falling short of

4

duties which are too vaguely implied in general notions of humanity and gentle behaviour. In such perplexity only experience or example can guide the instincts of the heart into reasonable channels. Now experience is not an advantage that everybody is free to acquire; it depends upon the various situations one has been placed in by destiny. Therefore for many people there remains only the example of others as a guiding principle in the practice of virtue.

It is precisely for such readers that works of this kind can be extremely useful, so long as they are written by a person of honour and good sense. Each event described therein is a kind of beacon, a lesson taking the place of experience; each adventure is a model upon which to form oneself: it has only to be adjusted to one's own circumstances. The whole work is a moral treatise entertainingly put into practice.

A serious reader may possibly be displeased at seeing me take up my pen again, at my time of life, in order to write an adventure story of love and fortune: but if the thoughts I have just expressed are well founded, they are my justification; if not, my error will be my excuse.

more accurate.

PART ONE

I MUST take you back to the time when I first met the Chevalier des Grieux. It was about six months before I left for Spain.[2] At that time I lived alone and seldom stirred abroad, but now and again I went on short journeys if my daughter wanted something attended to, and I made these as brief as I could. I once had to go to Rouen where she had asked me to see a case through the Law Courts relating to some land left by my maternal grandfather which I wished to hand over to her. On my way back I slept the first night at Evreux, and reached Pacy,[3] about five or six leagues further on, in time for dinner. As I came into the little town I was surprised to see all the people rushing out of their houses and gathering in a crowd outside a shabby-looking inn in front of which two covered wagons were standing. The two wagons had evidently only just arrived, for the horses were still panting and steaming in the shafts. I stopped a moment to find out the cause of the uproar, but I could get no sense out of the gaping crowd, who ignored my questions and kept on fighting their way towards the inn. But just then there appeared in the doorway a soldier, complete with bandolier and musket, and I beckoned him and asked him what all the excitement was about. 'Oh, it's nothing, Sir,' he said, 'just a dozen street-walkers that my friends and I are taking to Havre to be shipped off to America. Some of them aren't bad looking, either, and I suppose that's what these yokels want to see.' I might have left it at that and gone on my way if I had not been pulled up by the cries of an old woman who emerged from the inn wringing her hands and shouting that it was a wicked shame and enough to give anyone the horrors. 'What's the matter?' I asked. 'Oh, come and see, Sir! I tell you, it's enough to break your heart!' My

guides made to
have sympathy

curiosity was now thoroughly aroused, and I dismounted, left my horse with my man and forced my way through the crowd. It was certainly a pathetic sight that met my eyes: amongst the twelve women who were chained together by the waist in two rows of six was one whose face and bearing were so out of keeping with her present situation that in any other setting I would have taken her for a lady of the gentlest birth. She was in abject misery and her clothes were filthy, but all that had so little effect on her beauty that I felt nothing but pity and respect for her. She was trying to turn away as much as the chains would allow, so as to hide her face from us onlookers, and this effort at concealment was so natural that it seemed to come from feelings of modesty. The six guards escorting this party of outcasts were also in the room, and I took the one in charge aside and asked him to tell me something about this lovely girl. But he could give me nothing but a few bare facts. 'We picked her up from the Hôpital on police orders. I don't expect she was put in there for her good behaviour. I have questioned her more than once on the road but can't get a word out of her. But although I haven't got orders to treat her any better than the others, I seem to do little things for her because she looks a cut above them, somehow. There's a young fellow over there,' he added, 'who might be able to tell you more than I can about what has brought her down to this. He has followed her all the way from Paris. Crying nearly all the time, too. He must be her brother, or else a lover.'

I turned towards the corner and saw a young man sitting there, apparently unconscious of everything around him. I have never seen a more arresting picture of grief. His clothes were very plain, but a mere glance is all you need to gauge a man's birth and upbringing. As I went over to him he stood up, and I could see in his eyes, face and every movement such gentle refinement that I instinctively felt kindly disposed towards him. I sat down by his side. 'Please excuse my troubling you,' I said, 'but could you satisfy my curiosity? I should like to know that charming person over there. She does not look as if she were made for the sorry plight she is in.' He answered quite civilly

8

that he could not tell me who she was without giving away his own identity, and that he had the strongest reasons for wishing to remain unknown. 'But what I can tell you,' he went on, pointing to the guards, 'and those wretches know it all too well, is that I love her so passionately that she has made me the most unhappy man alive. I used every possible means in Paris to get her set free – petitions, intrigues, violence – nothing worked. And so I made up my mind to follow her, if need be to the ends of the earth. I shall embark with her and go to America. But,' he continued, returning to the subject of the guards, 'can you imagine anyone more inhuman than those foul creatures? They won't let me go near her. I had planned to attack them some leagues out from Paris, with the promised help of four men to whom I handed out a large sum. When it came to the fighting, they left me in the lurch and decamped with my money, and so, seeing that I could not succeed by force, I laid down my arms. Then I asked those guards to let me follow them, offering a handsome reward, of course. Their greed made them consent, but every time I have had permission to speak to her I have had to pay. My purse was soon empty, and now that I haven't a penny left the devils shove me back roughly whenever I take a step in her direction. Only a minute ago I made up my mind to brave their threats and go up to her, and they had the effrontery to raise the butts of their rifles at me. Now I shall have to sell the poor old horse that I have ridden up to now, so as to meet their demands and be able to finish the journey on foot.'

He seemed quite calm while he was telling me all this, but by the time he had finished there were tears in his eyes. The whole story struck me as one of the strangest and saddest I had ever heard. 'I don't want to press you to tell me your private business,' I said, 'but if I can help you in any way please take this as an offer.' 'I cannot see the faintest glimmer of hope,' he answered with a sigh. 'I have got to go through with it to the end. No, I shall go to America; at any rate I shall be free there with the woman I love. I have written to a friend of mine who will send me some help at Havre. The only trouble is to get that far and to find what alleviation I can on the way for this poor creature's sufferings.' As he spoke these words he glanced sorrowfully at his beloved. 'Look here,' I said, 'do let me put an end to your worries by giving you some money. I am sorry I cannot help you in any other way.' I managed to give him four louis without the guards noticing, for I was certain that they would put up their prices if they knew he had such a sum. It even occurred to me to strike a bargain with them so as to get permission for the young man to talk uninterruptedly to his love all the way to Havre. I beckoned again to the man in charge, who came over, and when I made the suggestion he seemed quite shamefaced, for all his brazen greed. 'You see, Sir,' he managed to stammer out, 'it isn't as though we refuse to let him talk to his girl, but he wants to be with her all the time, and that is a nuisance that ought to be paid for. It's only fair.' 'Well, how much do you want for not noticing it?' He had the effrontery to ask for two louis, but I handed them over without demur. 'But,' I said, 'mind you don't try on any tricks. I am going to give this gentleman my address so that he can let me know. And don't forget that I shall be in a position to have the matter followed up.' The affair cost me six louis altogether, but I could see that the young man deserved all my generosity, and his gratitude and the good grace with which he thanked me showed, if I needed any more showing, that he was a born gentleman. Before going out I had a word or two with the girl, and she sounded so charming and modest that I found myself making many a reflection on the inscrutable nature of woman. *Men find women incomprehensible*

I went back to my life of retirement and heard no more of this incident. Nearly two years went by, and I had forgotten it altogether, when a chance meeting led to my learning the whole story. On my way back from London with my pupil the Marquis of X, I had just reached Calais. We put up at the Golden Lion, if I remember rightly, and for various reasons we had to stay there all that day and the following night. During the afternoon I was walking along a street when I thought I recognized the young man I had seen at Pacy. He looked very shabby, and much paler

going to England

than when I had first seen him, and seemed to have just arrived in the town, for he was carrying an old portmanteau. But I at once remembered his face, which was too strikingly handsome to be easily forgotten. I said to the Marquis that we must go over and speak to him. When he recognized me he seized my hand and kissed it with unspeakable joy, saying how glad he was to have another chance of expressing his undying gratitude. I asked him where he had just come from and he answered that he had landed from Havre, where he had returned from America shortly before. 'You don't look too well off,' I said. 'Go along to the Golden Lion. That is where I am staying. I will join you there in a few minutes.' I hastened back there, full of impatience to hear the detailed story of his misfortunes and his journey to America. I treated him to every kindness and ordered everything to be done for his comfort. He needed no persuasion to tell me the story of his life. 'Sir,' he said, 'you have been so good to me that I should reproach myself with ingratitude if I kept anything back from you. I am prepared to acquaint you not only with my misfortunes and sufferings but also with my follies and shameful weakness. You will no doubt blame my behaviour but I am sure you will not be able to help pitying me.' *repentant sinner -*

At this point I must make it clear that I wrote down his story almost immediately after hearing it; consequently this narrative is perfectly accurate and faithful. By faithful I mean that it even reproduces comments and emotional digressions which the young fellow put in with the most natural ease of manner. This is his tale, and I shall add nothing to his own words, from beginning to end.

prodigal son returned back to native land.

I WAS seventeen and just at the end of my philosophy course at Amiens, where I had been sent by my parents, who belonged to one of the best families in P. My conduct at college had been so good and steady that the masters quoted me as an example to others. Not that I had made any particular efforts to deserve such praise, but I am quiet and gentle by disposition and studious by nature. Moreover a certain instinctive aversion from evil was credited to me as a positive virtue. All the best people in the town knew me and respected me for my birth, good looks and success at college. At my public oral examination[4] I made such an excellent impression that the bishop, who was present, suggested that I should embark on an ecclesiastical career, in which, he said, I would certainly go further than in the Order of Malta, which was what my family had planned for me. I already wore the Cross of Malta, and with it I was allowed the style of Chevalier des Grieux. As the vacation was beginning, I was getting ready to go home to my father who had promised to send me on to the Academy. My only regret at leaving Amiens was that it also meant leaving behind a friend from whom I had always been inseparable. He was a few years my senior and we had been brought up together, but as his family was poor he had no choice but to enter the priesthood and stay on in Amiens to take the necessary course of study. He was one of the very best of men, as you will see later in my story when you hear about his admirable qualities and his steadfast and generous friendship surpassing the most famous examples in antiquity. If only I had followed his advice at that time I should always have been good and happy. Or if I had listened to his criticisms when my passions were dragging me down to the abyss, I might at least have saved something from the wreck of my fortune and good name. But the only reward he has had has been the bitterness of seeing his loving care unavailing and more often than not brutally repulsed and taken for an insult and a nuisance.

I had arranged the date for leaving Amiens – how I wish I had fixed it a day earlier! I should have gone home to my father decent and clean. The day before I intended to leave I was walking along with my friend, whose name was Tiberge, when we saw the Arras coach⁵ arrive, and out of idle curiosity we followed it to the inn where passengers are set down. A few women got out and went straight indoors. But there was one very young one who waited alone in the inn-yard while an oldish man, who appeared to be in charge of her, was busy getting the luggage out of the boot. My modesty and reserve had been the admiration of all who knew me, and I had never so much as given a thought to the difference between the sexes, or more than a passing glance to any woman; but she seemed so lovely to me that then and there I was carried away by an overmastering passion. I had always suffered from the drawback of being over-shy and easily embarrassed, but far from being held back by this now I found myself confidently walking forward to meet the woman of my choice, the queen of my heart.

She was even younger than I was, but she was not in the least taken aback by the compliments I addressed to her. I asked her what brought her to Amiens and whether she knew anybody there. She answered quite simply that she had been sent there by her parents to become a nun. I had not been in love for more than a minute, but already love had so sharpened my wits that in a flash I made up my mind that such a project must not be allowed to blast my hopes. The way I spoke to her soon made her realize the state of my feelings, for she was much more experienced than I was. I gathered that she was being sent to the convent against her will, and I see now that it was probably to check the pleasure-loving tendencies that had already shown themselves in her, and that were to bring so much suffering on herself and me. I used all the arguments that awakening love and scholastic eloquence could devise to oppose her parents' inhuman plan. She made no pretence at haughtiness or severity, but remained silent for some time and then said that she knew quite well that she was going to be miserable, but that she supposed it must be God's will, since He had not shown her any other way out. Perhaps it was the soft appeal of her eyes as she spoke and her air of wistful sadness, or, more likely, it was the power of destiny luring me on to my destruction: at all events I did not hesitate a moment, but assured her that if she would rely on my honour and the deep affection I already felt for her, I was ready to devote my life to rescuing her from her tyrannical family and making her happy. On thinking it over since, I have been amazed time and again at my daring and the ease with which words came to me, but I suppose love would never have been called divine if it could not work miracles of this kind.

I went on to invent a hundred irresistible arguments, and my beautiful stranger knew quite well that men of my age are not deceivers. She confided to me that if I could see any means of setting her free she would feel she owed me gratitude for something dearer than life itself. I said again and again that I was ready to undertake anything, but being too inexperienced to think on the spur of the moment of any plan for helping her, I went no further than this general declaration, which was not very useful either to her or to me. At this juncture her old watchdog came back and all my hopes would have faded into thin air had she not had enough presence of mind for us both. To my surprise, when her manservant came up, I heard her referring to me as her cousin, and without seeming in the least disconcerted she told me that as she had been so fortunate as to meet me in Amiens she would postpone going into the convent for one day so as to have the pleasure of dining with me. I saw through her stratagem and played up well, suggesting that she put up at an inn the proprietor of which, having for many years been my father's coachman, had now set up on his own in Amiens. He would do anything for me. I escorted her there, the old chap muttering vaguely and Tiberge following on in silence with no idea what it was all about. He had not overheard our conversation as he had walked up and down the yard while I was holding forth about love to my fine lady, and now I got rid of him by inventing some errand for him to run. And so when we reached the inn I had the joy of being alone with my idol. In a very short time I realized that I was not nearly as callow as I thought. I had all sorts of pleasurable sensations the like of which I had never dreamed of before: a kind of ineffable warmth spread through my whole being and I experienced such over-powering emotion that for some time I could not utter a sound, but only let my passion declare itself through my eyes. Mademoiselle Manon Lescaut (she told me that was her name) seemed gratified by this proof of the power of her charms, and I thought she was as deeply affected as I was. She admitted that she would be overjoyed to owe her freedom to me, for she found me most charming. She then asked who I was, and when I told her, her affection visibly increased because, being of humbler birth, she felt flattered at having such a man as me for a lover. We discussed ways and means of belonging to each other, and after much thought agreed that the only way was to elope. The first thing was to dodge the watchful eye of her man, and, though he was only a hired servant, he was a person to be reckoned with. It was decided that I should hire a post-chaise during the night and bring it round to the inn very early before he woke up; then we would steal away, make straight for Paris and get married as soon as we arrived. I had all my savings, about fifty écus, and she had about twice as much. In our innocence we imagined that this sum would last for ever, and were confident that everything else would be equally satisfactory.

After the most delightful meal I had ever enjoyed, I went off to put the scheme into operation. Arrangements were all the easier because my things were ready packed for my return home next day. I had no trouble in getting my trunk moved and booking a chaise for five in the morning, the time when the city gates were opened; but the whole plan was nearly wrecked by an unexpected obstacle – Tiberge.

Although he was only three years older than I, Tiberge had a mature judgement in addition to his upright character, and, moreover, he loved me as a brother. The prettiness of Mademoiselle Manon, my eagerness to take her to her lodgings and, above all, the trouble I had taken to find a pretext for getting rid of him, gave him grounds for suspecting that I had fallen in love. He had not dared to return to the inn where he had left me, for fear of annoying me, but he had gone back to my lodgings, and he was still waiting there when I returned although it was ten o'clock at night. I was put out at finding him there, and he saw it, so he came straight to the point: 'I am sure you are planning something you want to hide from me. I can tell by the look of you.' I answered rather roughly that I was not obliged to account to him for all my plans. 'Perhaps not,' he went on, 'but so far you have always treated me as a friend, and as a friend I have a right to a little confidence and frankness.' He urged me to let him share my secret, and pleaded so long and so earnestly that, never having hidden anything from him before, I ended by taking him into my confidence about the whole affair. He heard me with such obvious disapproval that I trembled. I was particularly vexed at having so rashly divulged my intention to run away. He said that he was too intimate a friend of mine not to oppose the idea with all his might, and that he would begin by mustering all the reasons he could think of to dissuade me. But if I did not give up such an absurd notion he would go and warn somebody in a position to stop me. Thereupon he read me a lecture lasting over a quarter of an hour, finishing up by renewed threats to inform against me unless I gave him my word of honour to behave more reasonably. I was furious at having given the game away at such an awkward moment. But in those two or three hours love had taught me many things, and now it occurred to me that I had not mentioned that the project was to be carried out the very next day. So I decided to deceive him by prevarication. 'Tiberge,' I said, 'so far I have assumed that you were my friend, and I wanted to test you by letting you into this secret. It is quite true that I am in love, I have not deceived you over that; but as to the elopement idea, that is not the sort of thing to be rushed through without careful thought. Come and call for me tomorrow at nine, and if it can be managed I will let you see her. You shall then judge for yourself whether she is worthy of the step I am contemplating.' This speech called forth many friendly protestations on his part, and he left me alone.

I spent all night settling my affairs, and at dawn I found Mademoiselle Manon waiting for me at the inn. She was stationed at her window, which looked on to the street, and, as soon as she saw me, stole down and opened the door herself. We got away without a sound. I carried the bundle of clothes which was all she had by way of luggage. The chaise was ready to leave and in a moment we were speeding away from the town.[6] I will tell you later what Tiberge did when he found that I had tricked him. My treatment of him in no way lessened his determination to do his best for me. You will see the lengths to which he went and how bitterly I was to regret my persistent ingratitude.

Manon and I made such good speed that we were at Saint-Denis before nightfall. I had galloped by the side of the chaise and we had had no chance of talking except during the stops for changing horses, but now that Paris and safety were so near, we allowed ourselves time to eat something, as we had had nothing since leaving Amiens. Passionately as I loved her, she found ways of showing me that her love for me was no less passionate, and we cared so little about other people that we gave ourselves up to our embraces without waiting to be alone. The postillions and the folk at the inn looked on with amazement, and I noticed that they were surprised to see such transports of love in two youngsters of our age. All our ideas about marriage were forgotten at Saint-Denis; we tricked the Church of its rights, and before we had given the matter a thought found ourselves man and wife. I am quite sure that with my loyal and affectionate nature I should have been happy for life with Manon if only she had been faithful to me. The better I got to know her, the more charms of mind, heart, character and above all beauty I discovered in her, and her manifold and ever-fresh attractions bound

17

me to her by ties so strong yet so delightful that I should have been content never to break them. What a terrible change of fortune was to be mine! Those very things which have brought me to despair might have made me rapturously happy, and I have become the most wretched man alive through that very constancy of mine which might have brought me the ineffable joys of true love.

We took furnished rooms in Paris, in the Rue V.[7] As ill-luck would have it, we were quite near the house of M. de B., the notorious tax-farmer. Three weeks went by, weeks of such delirious passion that I scarcely gave a thought to my family and the sorrow my disappearance must have given my father. But as my love was not as yet sullied by debauchery, and as Manon behaved with much circumspection, we lived in a peaceful atmosphere that gradually recalled me to a sense of duty. In this frame of mind I decided to seek a reconciliation with my father. Manon was so enchanting that it seemed to me she could not fail to please him, if only I could find a way of telling him about her many qualities: in short, I imagined that I could get his permission to marry her, having found that I could not do so without his consent. I spoke about it to Manon, and gave her to understand that, apart altogether from motives of filial duty, sheer necessity might soon come into the picture because our funds were running low and I was beginning to revise my opinion that they were inexhaustible.

Manon heard this news with marked coolness. But as the objections she raised were based on her affection for me and the fear that when my father had found out our hiding-place he would lose me, if he did not come round to our point of view, I had not the slightest suspicion of the cruel blow being prepared for me at that very moment. She countered the argument of financial necessity by saying that we still had enough left for several weeks, and that after that she would write to some relatives in the country from whom she was sure she could manage to wheedle some money. And her refusal was softened by such tender caresses that I could not entertain the least doubt about her love, but even applauded all her arguments and plans. As I lived for her alone, how could I do otherwise?

I had left the management of our exchequer and the running of our daily life entirely to her. Soon after this conversation, I noticed that we were living in a much better style and that she had some new and quite expensive clothes. As I knew that we could not have much more than twelve or fifteen pistoles left, I let her see how surprised I was at this obvious improvement in our position. She laughed, told me not to worry and said: 'Didn't I promise you I would find the wherewithal?' I loved her too singleheartedly to be easily disturbed by suspicions.

One afternoon I went out, having warned her that I would be away longer than usual. When I came back I was surprised to be kept waiting two or three minutes at the door. We had but one servant-girl of about our own age, and when at length she opened the door I asked her why she had been so long. She mumbled some tale about never having heard a knock. As I had only knocked once I said: 'But if you didn't hear me, why have you opened the door now?' She was so taken aback at this that she lost her head altogether and began to cry. It was not her fault, she explained; Madame had ordered her not to open the door until M. de B. had gone down by the other staircase that connected directly with our private room. I was so staggered that I could not find the courage to enter the flat, but murmured something about important business and ran downstairs again, ordering the girl to tell her mistress that I would soon be back but not to say that she had mentioned M. de B.

I was almost dazed as I went down the stairs, and there were tears running down my cheeks, though I had no idea why I was crying. I went into the nearest café, sat at a table, buried my face in my hands and tried to sort out my conflicting emotions. I scarcely dared recall what I had just heard, but tried to think it was some illusion, and once or twice nearly went back to the flat intending to act as though nothing had happened. It seemed so impossible that Manon had deceived me that I felt it was insulting even to suspect her. I worshipped her; that was certain, and she had returned my love no less ardently. How could I accuse her of being any less sincere and loyal than I had been? What possible reason could she have for deceiving me? Scarcely three hours before she had lavished the most affectionate caresses on me, and had received mine with every appearance of passionate abandon. I felt that I could be as sure of her heart as I was of my own. 'No, no,' I kept on saying to myself, 'it can't be true. She could never betray me, for she knows that I live for her alone, that I adore her. There is nothing in that to make her hate me.'

And yet – how could I explain M. de B.'s visit, and especially his furtive departure? And what about Manon's little luxuries, which certainly went far beyond our present means? It all smacked of the generosity of a new lover. How else could I explain the confident way she relied on resources I must know nothing about? I was hard put to it to find as favourable an answer to these riddles as I should have liked. But on the other hand she had scarcely been out of my sight since we came to Paris. In the daily round, out on walks or at the theatre, we had always been together for the simple reason that we could not endure to be parted for a moment. We had had to keep on declaring love to each other for fear of dying of anxiety. In short, I could scarcely remember a minute when Manon could have had dealings with anyone but me. At last I thought I had found the clue to the mystery. Of course, I said to myself, M. de B. was a man of far-reaching business connexions, and no doubt Manon's relatives had used him as an agent for letting her have some money; she must have had some from him already and today he must have brought another instalment. All this secrecy, then? Simply a little joke of hers, so as to give me a nice surprise. Maybe she would have told me all about it if I had gone home in a normal manner instead of coming here to mope. Anyhow, she will not conceal it now, if I mention it myself.

By dint of repeating this theory to myself, I managed to stifle most of my forebodings. I went straight home, embraced Manon as though nothing were amiss, and she greeted me quite naturally. My first impulse was to let her know what I had guessed (and now I felt more sure than ever that I was right), but I held back in the hope that she would make the first move and tell me everything that had happened.

Supper was brought in, and I sat down gaily enough. The candle was on the table between us, and as it lit up her face I thought there was an uneasy look in her eyes. This uneasiness began to affect me too. I noticed that she was looking at me with an unusual expression, whether it was love or pity I could not tell, but there was something gentle and sad about it. I studied her face just as attentively as she did mine, and possibly she was equally puzzled about what was going on in my mind. Neither of us touched any food or said a word. And then I saw that her eyes were shining with tears – treacherous tears!

'Ah, dearest Manon,' I cried, 'you are weeping, you are moved to tears, and you won't tell me anything about your troubles.' But she answered by heaving sighs which only added to my apprehension. I rose from table and begged her with all the tender solicitude of love to say why she was crying. I felt more dead than alive, and even while drying her tears I was weeping myself. The hardest heart would have melted at these signs of my grief and fear. While I was wholly concerned with her in this way, I heard some footsteps on the stairs. Somebody tapped softly on the door. Manon gave me a kiss, wrenched herself out of my arms, ran quickly into the other room and shut the door behind her. For a moment I imagined that she did not want the strangers to see the state she was in. I opened the outer door. Scarcely had I done so before I was seized by three men whom I recognized as my father's lackeys. They did not rough-handle me, but two of them pinioned my arms while the third went through my pockets and removed the only weapon I had on me, a small knife. They apologized for being obliged to show me such scant respect, and explained, of course, that they were acting on my father's orders and that my elder brother was waiting for me down below in a carriage. I was so taken by surprise that I let them lead me away without question or protest. Sure enough my brother was waiting in the carriage and I was put next to him. The coachman, who already had his orders, drove us at full speed to Saint-Denis. My brother embraced me with every sign of affection but did not say a word, so that I had all the leisure I needed for thinking things over.

At first it all seemed so confused that I could see no daylight at all. Clearly I had been heartlessly betrayed, but by whom? Tiberge was the first to come to mind. 'You wretch,' I thought to myself, 'it's all up with you if my suspicions prove true!' But then I recollected that he did not know my address, so it could not have been obtained through him. I could not bring myself to accuse Manon. True, the strange mood of sadness which she had been unable to shake off, her tears and the tender kiss she had given me as she ran off, were all so many mysteries, but I was inclined to put all that down to some presentiment of disaster for us both, and even while I was deploring the accident that had torn me away from her, I was simple enough to fancy that at that very moment she was more to be pitied than I. After much cogitation I came to the conclusion that I must have been seen in the streets of Paris by some acquaintances who had passed the information on to my father. This thought comforted me, for I counted on getting out of it with some slight punishment or perhaps merely a few heavy paternal homilies. I resolved to bear everything patiently and promise to do anything I was asked, so as to make it easier to return at once to Paris and restore life and joy to my own Manon.

We soon reached Saint-Denis. My brother ascribed my strange silence to fear, and tried to cheer me up by assuring me that father's severity need have no terrors for me provided I was ready to be tractable, dutiful and worthy of his love. But at Saint-Denis he took the precaution of making the three lackeys sleep in the same room with me. It was humiliating to find myself at the same inn where I had stopped with Manon on our journey from Amiens to Paris. The host and the servants recognized me, put two and two together and guessed my story. I overheard the host saying: 'It's the pretty young gentleman who called here six weeks ago with the little girl he was so taken with! Wasn't she a beauty! And didn't they make love, poor kids!

22

Well, I say it's a pity they've been parted.' I pretended not to have heard, and kept out of sight as much as possible. At Saint-Denis my brother had a small chaise waiting and we set off in it very early the next morning, reaching home in the evening of the next day. He went and saw my father first and told him how willingly I had let myself be brought home, and thanks to his intervention on my behalf I was welcomed less unkindly than I had expected. Father indulged in a few general reprimands about my having absented myself without permission. Concerning my mistress, he said that I had deserved what had befallen me for having let myself fall into the clutches of an unknown woman; that he had thought me more prudent, but hoped that this little adventure would make me more sensible. I chose to interpret this speech in the way that fitted in best with my own ideas, thanked him for his kind forgiveness and promised to behave with obedience and circumspection. But in my heart I was already triumphant, for as things were turning out I was certain that I should be able to escape from the house, probably even that very night.

We sat down to supper, and I was chaffed a good deal on the 'conquest' I had made at Amiens and on my elopement with such a faithful mistress. But I took these barbed shafts in good part and was even rather glad of the chance they gave me to talk freely about what was continually on my mind. Suddenly, however, something father said made me prick up my ears. He mentioned perfidy and paid services on the part of M. de. B. This name gave me a shock and I begged him to explain in more detail. He turned to my brother and asked him if he had not told me the whole story. My brother answered that on the journey I had seemed so quiet that he had not thought I needed such a remedy to cure me of my folly. My father appeared to be hesitating as to whether he should go on with his explanations, but I urged him to do so with such insistence that he satisfied me, or rather tortured me with a most horrible tale.

He began by asking me whether I was still gullible enough to believe that this woman loved me. I made so bold as to declare that I was quite sure she did and that nothing could ever shake that belief. He roared with laughter. 'Ha, ha, ha!' he cried, 'that's lovely! A fine fool you are, I must say, and it's nice to see you in this frame of mind. You know, my boy, it's really a pity to put you into the Order of Malta; you've got all the ingredients for a most long-suffering and complaisant husband.' And he added various other witticisms in the same style on what he called my silly credulity. As I made no attempt to speak, he went on to say that, according to calculations he had made, Manon had loved me for about twelve days after our departure from Amiens. 'I know,' he said, 'that you left Amiens on the 28th of last month. It is now the 29th of this month. It is eleven days since M. de. B. wrote to me. Let us suppose it took him eight days to get to know your lady friend properly. So if we take eleven and eight from the thirty-one between the 28th of last month and the 29th of this, we get twelve, or thereabouts.' More roars of laughter. I was so overcome that I was afraid I should never hold out until the end of this wretched comedy; but father began talking again: 'You had better know, since you don't seem to, that M. de B. has won your princess's heart. It's all nonsense for him to make out that he wanted to get you away from her out of purely disinterested regard for my feelings. Just as though we could expect such noble sentiments from a man of his sort. Why, he doesn't even know me! He found out from her who your father was, and simply to get rid of you he wrote giving me your address and an account of your goings-on, taking care to give me to understand that force would be needed to make sure of you. He offered to find means of laying hands on you, and your brother caught you napping on information supplied by him and the lady herself. Now pat yourself on the back on your long success. You can conquer pretty quickly, my son, but you don't know how to safeguard your conquests.'

I could not stand any more of this speech, every word of which pierced me to the heart. I got up and made for the door, but had only taken a few steps when I collapsed on the floor in a dead faint. I was quickly revived, but only to fall into paroxysms of weeping, interspersed with lamentations and heartrending cries. My father did his utmost to console me, for he was really very fond of me. I heard his voice but did not follow what he was saying, and in the end I begged him on bended knee and with clasped hands to let me go back to Paris and give M. de B. what he deserved. 'No,' I said, 'he has never won her love; he has forced her to it; he has seduced her by some charm or even drug; he may have violated her. Manon loves me, I am certain of that. He must have threatened her at the dagger's point to make her give me up. Oh God! could it be possible that Manon betrayed me or has ceased to care for me?'

My father realized that, in my present state of mind, nothing would stop me trying to carry out my repeated threats to rush straight back to Paris. I even kept trying to jump up and do so there and then. And so he took me to a room at the top of the house and left two servants to keep an eye on me. I was frantic; I would have given up life itself a thousand times for just one quarter of an hour in Paris, but I saw that I had given myself away so unmistakably that I would not be allowed to leave that room. I had a look at the distance from the windows to the ground, and saw at once that there was no escaping that way. So I tried cajoling the two servants, swearing to make their fortunes some day if they would let me slip away. But arguments, wheed-lings, threats were in vain, and I gave up all hope, determined to die, and threw myself on the bed intending never to leave it alive. All that night and all the following day I refused the food that was brought me. In the afternoon my father came up to see me and did everything he could to comfort me, enjoining me with such urgency to eat something that I did so out of respect for his authority. For several days I ate nothing except when he was present and had to be obeyed. He persevered in finding arguments calculated to bring me back to my senses and make me see the faithlessness of the despicable Manon. It is quite true that by then I had ceased to respect her virtue – how could I respect anyone so fickle and disloyal? But her picture, her lovely features, were imprinted on my mind for ever. Yet I was not deceived. 'I may die,' I said, 'and I deserve to die after so much

25

shame and suffering, but if I died a thousand deaths how could I ever forget my heartless Manon?'

My father was astonished to see how profoundly I was affected. Knowing how honourable my principles were, and feeling certain that I must therefore scorn her for her baseness, he came to the conclusion that my constancy must come not so much from this particular passion as from a taste for women in general. He took so much to this idea that one day, prompted solely by his desire to see me happy, he sounded me about it. 'My boy,' he said, 'until now I had proposed to put you into the Order of Malta, but it is plain that your natural inclinations do not lie in that direction. You are fond of pretty women. I think we shall have to find one to your liking. Tell me frankly what you think about it.' I answered that I had ceased to draw any distinction between women, and that after my bitter experience I hated them all alike. He smiled and said, 'I will find you one like Manon, but more dependable.' 'If you really want to help me,' I said, 'you must give her back to me. Believe me, father, she has not betrayed me, she is incapable of anything so base and cruel. I am sure that it is this treacherous B. who has tricked all three of us, you, her and me. If only you knew how affectionate and straightforward she is – I mean, if you really knew her – you would love her yourself.'

'What a baby you are!' he replied. 'How can you be so blind, after all I have told you about her? She handed you over to your brother herself, I tell you. You ought to put even her name out of your mind and have the sense to make the best of my leniency.' I realized all too clearly that he was right, but some involuntary impulse made me still want to take her part. 'Ah! yes,' I went on after a pause, 'it is all too true that I am the wretched dupe of the meanest of tricks. Yes, I agree that I must still be only a baby, for they found it the easiest thing in the world to exploit my gullibility. But I know what to do for revenge.' My father wanted to know what I meant. 'I shall go to Paris,' I said, 'set fire to B.'s house and burn him and Manon alive.' There were tears of mortification running down my cheeks; this silly outburst made my father laugh again and only made him redouble his vigilance.

I was imprisoned in this way for six whole months. The first
month saw little change in my state of mind. I continually alter-
nated between extremes of hate and love, hope and despair,
according to the particular memory of Manon that came uppermost in my mind. Half the time I conjured up a vision of her as
the most lovable of women and longed with all my heart to see her
again, but the other half I saw her as a vicious and deceitful whore
and resolved with all sorts of oaths to hunt her out and punish her.
But in time I began to read the books that were given me, and
reading brought back a certain amount of calm. I re-read all the
great authors and widened my field of knowledge by adding new
ones. My old taste for study returned, and you will see later what
use I was to make of it. My own experience of love opened my eyes
to the meaning of many a passage in Horace and Virgil which had
always been obscure before. I wrote a sentimental commentary on
the fourth book of the *Aeneid*; I still hope to publish it and venture
to think the public will find it interesting. As I worked on it I
reflected that what the hapless Dido needed was a heart like mine.

One day Tiberge came to see me in my prison. The warmth of
his affection quite took me by surprise, for so far I had not had
any proofs of his feelings towards me which justified my thinking
of them as anything more than the usual college friendship which
springs up between young fellows of about the same age. In the
five or six months since I had last seen him, he had developed
and matured so much that his expression and tone of voice
commanded my respect. He spoke more like a wise counsellor
than a school friend, deploring my excesses and welcoming my
recovery which he thought well under way. He finished by
exhorting me to learn from this youthful indiscretion and open
my eyes to the vanity of all sensual pleasures. But at this point he
noticed the astonishment in my face, for he went on: 'My dear
fellow, I am saying nothing that is not founded on solid truth,
and I have only reached this conviction after long and careful
thought. There was a time when I was as much given to sensual
gratification as you are, but God also gave me a love of virtue. I
used my intelligence and compared the fruits of sin with those of

virtue, and, God helping me, I soon found out the difference. The world has no charms for me now. Can you guess what has kept me in the world and prevented me from seeking the peace of the solitary life? Simply my friendship for you. I know your qualities of heart and mind and that there is no good thing you are not capable of. The lust of the flesh has led you astray, and what a loss it has been for the forces of good! Your flight from Amiens was such a grievous shock to me that I have not had a moment's happiness since. You can tell the truth of that by all the things I have felt impelled to do. Listen.'

He told me how, after realizing that I had deceived him and gone off with Manon, he had taken horse to follow me, but as we had four or five hours' start he had found it impossible to overtake me. Nevertheless he had reached Saint-Denis only half an hour after I had left. Being fairly certain that I would stay in Paris, he had spent six weeks vainly searching for me; he had been to all the places where he thought I might be found, and eventually one day he had recognized Manon in a theatre. She was so gorgeously attired that he thought she must owe such opulence to a new lover. He had followed her carriage home and found out from a servant that she was being kept by M. de B. 'But I didn't leave it at that,' he continued. 'I went back there the next day to find out from her what had become of you. As soon as I mentioned your name she rudely turned her back on me, and I had to return to the country without finding out anything else. There I heard of your adventure and of your subsequent breakdown, but I did not want to see you until I was sure of finding you calmer.'

'So you have seen Manon!' I answered. 'You are luckier than I am, for I am doomed never to set eyes on her again.' And I heaved a sigh. That sigh revealed how little resistance I had as far as she was concerned, and he did not like it, but he adroitly diverted the talk to the flattering subject of my character and real inclinations, and he did it so well that, even during that first visit of his, I began to conceive a strong desire to give up all worldly pleasures and, like him, enter the priesthood.

So strongly did this idea appeal to me that my mind came back to it whenever I was alone. I recalled the same advice that had been given to me by the bishop of Amiens, and the glowing picture he had painted of my prospects if I made up my mind to go into the Church. But these meditations of mine were not without a certain admixture of genuine piety. I resolved to lead a good Christian life devoted to study and religion, which would leave me no time to dally with dangerous visions of love. I would scorn what most men admire, and as the desires of my heart were henceforth to be founded on reason and respect alone, I should have as few worries as desires. Along these lines I mapped out a plan for the peaceful and solitary life. The ingredients included a sequestered cottage with a little copse and a babbling brook at the end of the garden, a library of choice books, a select number of virtuous and intellectual friends and good but frugal and wholesome fare. I threw in a literary correspondence with a friend in Paris who kept me informed about the news – not so much to gratify my idle curiosity as to entertain me with the distant spectacle of the vain and feverish pursuits of men. 'What bliss will be mine!' I thought, 'and will not all my ambitions be satisfied?' These projects were calculated to flatter all my natural tendencies. But when all these sage deliberations were over, I felt that there was something still wanting, and that to make this peaceful retirement delightful beyond all possibility of improvement Manon would have to be there.

Meanwhile Tiberge frequently came to see me and did his best to encourage me to follow up the plan he had suggested, and I seized a chance to broach the matter with my father. He declared that he wished to leave his children a free choice of career and that, whatever I were to decide, he would not interfere but only give me his advice. And the advice he gave me was very wise and, far from turning me away from my project, it made me go into it with my eyes open. It was almost time for the beginning of the academic year, and I agreed with Tiberge that we would go up together to the seminary of Saint-Sulpice, where he could finish his theology and I could start mine. He was very well thought of by the bishop of our diocese, and through him he was awarded a generous grant before we left.

THINKING I had now quite recovered, my father raised no objections to letting me go. We went to Paris, where the cassock took the place of the Cross of Malta and the style of Abbé des Grieux that of Chevalier. I took to my studies so diligently that in a few months I made rapid strides. By dint of working all day and half the night, I acquired such a reputation that people already began to congratulate me on the swift advancement I could not fail to get, and without my having made any move myself my name was put down on the list of livings to be awarded. Nor did I neglect the devotional side, but took part in all the religious exercises with fervent piety. Tiberge was so overjoyed with what he looked upon as his handiwork, that more than once I saw tears in his eyes when he spoke of what he called my conversion. All human resolutions are subject to change: that in itself has never surprised me, for they are born of a passion and another passion may destroy them. But when I think of the purity of the resolves which led me to Saint-Sulpice, and the deep inner peace which God poured into my soul as I carried them out, I am appalled at the ease with which I broke them. If it be true that Heaven always gives us strength equal to that of our passions, how can we explain the terrible power which can suddenly carry us far away from our duty, stripping us of all strength to resist and all feelings of remorse? I thought I was saved for ever from the weakness of love; I imagined that I should always prefer reading a page of St Augustine or a quarter of an hour's pious meditation to all the pleasures of the senses, even those that Manon might give. And yet one accursed moment plunged me back into the abyss, and my fall was all the more irreparable because, when I found myself brought as low as I had been before, new excesses dragged me even further down.

I had been in Paris nearly a year without attempting to find out what had become of Manon. At first this had cost me a considerable effort, but I managed to conquer the temptation thanks to the unfailing advice of Tiberge and my own common sense. The later months went by so peacefully that I thought I was on the point of forgetting that lovely, fickle creature for ever. The time came for me to make my public oration in the school of theology, and I invited several distinguished people to honour me with their presence.[8] This made my name known all over Paris, and it even reached the ears of my former mistress. She did not recognize it for certain under its new style of abbé, but her curiosity was aroused by a name so similar to mine, though whether it was from some lingering feeling of interest or, perhaps, compunction for her deceitful treatment of me I have never been able to decide. At all events, she came to the Sorbonne with some other ladies, was present at my discourse and doubtless recognized me at once.

I had no idea that she was there. You know that in that hall there are some private alcoves for ladies, where they can sit behind a curtain. At six o'clock I returned to Saint-Sulpice, covered with glory and complimented on all sides. A moment after I had got back I was told that a lady was asking to see me and I went straight to the parlour. God! What did I see? Manon herself. Manon, more dazzlingly beautiful than I had ever known her. She was not yet eighteen and her loveliness was then beyond description. Such gentle grace, yet at the same time such vivacity and subtle charm – she looked like the incarnation of love itself. Every line of her face was enchanting.

I stood as though petrified, and waited, trembling and not daring to look at her, hoping that she would explain the purpose of her visit. For a time she seemed as embarrassed as I was, but at length, seeing that I was not going to break my silence, she began in faltering tones and with one hand held over her eyes as though to hide her tears. She admitted that her infidelities merited my hatred, but went on to say that if it were true that I had ever

cared for her, it was very unfeeling of me to have let two years
go by without troubling to find out what had become of her,
and still more cruel to see her now in front of me in such a
pitiful condition and not say a word. As I stood listening to her
the ferment within my soul was indescribable.

She sat down, but I remained standing, half turning away
from her, not daring to look her straight in the eyes. Over and
over again I began to say something but could not finish a
sentence. At last, by dint of a supreme effort, I shouted rather
than said: 'Manon, you devil, oh you deceitful devil!' She
repeated, amid floods of tears, that she was not trying to justify
her abominable behaviour. 'What do you want, then?' I cried. 'I
want to die,' she answered, 'unless you give me back your love,
for without that I cannot live.' 'Then why don't you ask for my
life?' I said, now weeping too, in spite of myself; 'ask for my life,
which is all I have left to give you, for you have had my love all
along.' Scarcely were these words out of my mouth before she
leaped up, flung her arms round me and smothered me with
caresses, calling me all those magical names which love invents
in its most frenzied moments of passion. I only half responded,
for I was horror-stricken at the contrast between the serenity of
but a few moments ago and the wild stirrings of desire I could
already feel within me. I was shuddering as you do when you
find yourself alone at night on some desolate moorland, when all
familiar bearings are lost and a panic fear comes over you that
you can dispel only by calmly studying all the landmarks.

We sat down together, I took her hands in mine and looked at
her with despair in my eyes. 'Oh, Manon,' I said, 'I never
expected my love to be repaid with such black ingratitude. It was
not hard for you to deceive a man you had so completely under
your spell, who thought himself supremely happy if he could but
please and obey. Tell me, have you found any other man so
loving and devoted? No, I do not think so; nature has not made
many of my temper. Will you at least say whether you have
missed me sometimes? How much trust can I put in this sudden
fit of kindness that has sent you back today to console me? It

is easy enough to see that you are lovelier than ever, but, in the name of all I have suffered for you, tell me, Manon, will you be truer this time?'

She expressed her penitence in such pathetic terms, and swore to be true with so many oaths and protestations, that she touched my heart and stirred me to the depths of my being. 'Dearest Manon,' I said, in a profane mixture of amorous and theological language, 'you are too adorable for a mortal creature. I can feel my heart being carried aloft in a triumph of ecstasy. All the talk about liberty here at Saint-Sulpice is sheer nonsense. I am going to throw away my career and good name for you – yes I know I am, I can read it in your eyes – but what sacrifices will not be fully repaid by your love? Fortune's favours have no charms for me, honour and glory are mere will o' the wisps; all my clerical ambitions were vain imaginings; all possessions, except what I hope to share with you, are worthless because they carry no weight in my heart against one glance from your eyes.'

And yet, although I promised to forgive and forget all her frailties, I felt I must know all about how she had been seduced by M. de B. I learned that he had seen her at the window, desired her passionately, and wooed her in true farmer-general style, that is to say by stating in a letter that payment would be in proportion to favours received. She had yielded first of all with no other object than to get out of him some large sum that would keep us both comfortably. Then he had held out in front of her such dazzling promises that she had given in little by little, and (she said) I could tell how bitterly she regretted doing so by the grief I had seen on her face just before our separation. In spite of the luxury with which he had surrounded her she had never tasted any real pleasure with him, not only because he had none of my delicacy and refinement of manner, but because, in the midst of all the amusements he constantly lavished on her, in her heart of hearts she had never ceased to have a haunting memory of my love and a growing sense of guilt for her unfaithfulness. She told me about Tiberge and how his visit had embarrassed her. 'I could have stood up better to a stab in the heart,' she said, 'and I turned my back on him because I could not face him even for one moment.'

She went on to tell me how she had found out that I was in Paris and about my change of condition and examination at the Sorbonne. I gathered that during my public disputation she had had the greatest difficulty in withholding not only her tears but even audible sobs and groans, so deeply had she been moved. She had stayed behind until last so that nobody should see her emotion, and then, acting on a sudden irresistible impulse, she had come straight to the seminary with a mind to die there if I refused to forgive her.

What heart of stone would not have been softened by such a touching proof of bitter remorse? For my part I felt at that moment that I would have given up all the bishoprics in Christendom for Manon. I asked her what steps we ought to take next, and she said that first and foremost we must get out of the seminary and think things out in some safer place. I fell in with all her wishes without question. She drove in her carriage to the corner of the street and waited there, while I slipped out and joined her a minute later without having been noticed by the doorkeeper. We began by going to a wardrobe dealer's, where I resumed the braided coat and sword, Manon paying for everything as I had not a penny (for fear of anything happening to prevent my getting out of Saint-Sulpice, she had not allowed me to go back to my room even for a moment to get my money). In any case my fortune was very modest, while thanks to the liberality of M. de B. she was rich enough to think nothing of what she was making me leave behind. While we were still in the shop we had a conference about what we should do next.

She announced her intention of making a clean break with M. de B. This was calculated to make me appreciate the full value of what she was prepared to give up for me. 'I am willing to leave him all his furniture,' she said; 'the things are his anyway, but it is only right that I should take the jewellery and close on sixty thousand francs I have got out of him in these two years. I haven't given him any hold over me, and so we can stay in Paris without any danger and take a nice house where we shall live happily ever after.'

I pointed out that even if there were no danger for her in Paris there was a great deal for me, for I was bound to be recognized sooner or later and would always run the risk of repeating the experience I had already had. But she gave me to understand that she would be reluctant to leave Paris, and I was so afraid of upsetting her that there were no risks I was not willing to scorn so long as she were pleased. However, we found a compromise, which was to rent a house in some village on the outskirts from which it would be easy to go into town for business or pleasure whenever we wanted. We decided on Chaillot, which is not far out. Manon went straight home and I made for the little gate of the Tuileries garden, where I was to wait for her.

She came back an hour later in a cab, with her maid and some trunks containing her clothes and valuables. We were soon at Chaillot, where we put up for the first night at a hotel in order to have time to look for a house or, failing that, a convenient flat. We found something to our liking the very next day.

At first I thought that my happiness was built on unshakable foundations. Manon was sweetness and kindness itself, and the many thoughtful little attentions with which she surrounded me seemed more than a reward for all my troubles. As by now we had both had a little experience of life, we gave some thought to our financial position. Our capital of sixty thousand francs was not likely to last for a long lifetime, but neither were we inclined to cut down our expenditure too drastically. Economy was not Manon's outstanding quality any more than it was mine. This was the plan I suggested: 'Sixty thousand francs,' I said, 'might keep us going for ten years.[9] If we stay at Chaillot we can manage on two thousand écus a year. We shall be able to live a respectable but simple life, and our main outgoings will be on theatres and the up-keep of a carriage. We must work it out systematically: you are fond of the Opera; we can go twice a week, and as for gaming, we must control it so that our losses never exceed two pistoles. It is most unlikely that ten years will not bring about some change in my family; my father is old and may die, and then I shall have some property and we shall be at the end of all our anxieties.'

If only we had had the wisdom to keep to it closely, this arrangement would certainly not have been the silliest one I had made in my life. But our resolutions lasted little more than a month. Manon was pleasure-mad and I was mad on her. Some new reason for spending money arose at every moment, and far from regretting the sums she squandered I was the first to buy her anything she fancied. Even our home at Chaillot began to get on her nerves, for with the approach of winter everybody went back to town and the country was deserted. She suggested taking a house in Paris again. I did not agree, but in order to give her some satisfaction I said that we might take furnished rooms there. It would be somewhere to spend the night when we stayed late at the assembly-rooms where we went several evenings a week – her pretext for wanting to leave Chaillot was the difficulty of getting home late at night. So now we had two homes, one in town and the other in the country, and this change promptly led to the final breakdown of our affairs, because it was directly responsible for two adventures which brought disaster.

Manon had a brother in the Lifeguards. Unfortunately for us his lodgings in Paris were in the same street as ours. One morning he saw his sister at the window, recognized her and made straight for our rooms. He was a coarse, unprincipled scoundrel. He burst into our room swearing horribly, and as he knew something of his sister's way of life he spared her neither insults nor foul names. I had gone out a moment before, which was perhaps as well for him or for me, as I was not prepared to put up with insults. I came back just after he had gone, and I could tell by the state Manon was in that something very untoward had happened. She described the distressing scene she had just gone through and her brother's brutal threats. I was so enraged that I would have rushed off there and then to take revenge had I not been held back by her tears, and, moreover, while we were still talking about him, he came back into the room unannounced. If I had known him I would not have received him as civilly as I did, but having greeted us with an ingratiating smile he plunged straight

36

into an apology to Manon for his fit of temper. He had had a mistaken impression, so he said, that she was living an irregular life, and this had made him angry, but he had inquired of one of our servants who I was and had heard such glowing accounts of me that he wanted to be on good terms with us. It was somewhat strange and disconcerting to hear that he had had this information from one of my lackeys, but I accepted the compliment with a fairly good grace in order to please Manon. She seemed delighted to see her brother in such a conciliatory mood, and we asked him to stay to dinner. In a very short time he made himself so much at home that, when he heard us mention returning to Chaillot, he insisted on going with us. We had to give him a seat in our carriage. It was like an official entry into possession. He soon developed such an affection for us that he made our home his own and took over control of all our belongings. He called me his brother, and, using as an excuse the freedom that exists between brothers, he considered himself entitled to bring all his friends to our Chaillot home and entertain them at our expense. He fitted himself out with sumptuous clothes and had the bills sent to us. He even pledged our name to pay his debts. I shut my eyes to this barefaced exploitation so as not to displease Manon, and even pretended not to notice that from time to time he was relieving her of large sums in cash. True, being a born gambler, he had the good faith to give her a share in any bit of good luck that came his way, but our own resources were by now too slender to cope for any length of time with such extravagant outgoings. I was on the point of having a very clear explanation with him so as to put an end to his importunities, when a disastrous accident saved me this trouble by inflicting another one on us which ruined us beyond all hope of recovery.

One night we had slept in Paris, as we often did. In the morning our servant, who on these occasions stayed alone at Chaillot, came and told me that fire had broken out in my house during the night and had been extinguished only with great difficulty. I asked her whether the furniture had been damaged, and she said that there had been such confusion, owing to the crowds of folk who had come offering help, that she could not be sure of anything. I trembled for our money which was kept in a little coffer, and went off to Chaillot with all speed. No need to hurry: it had already gone.

At that moment I understood how you can love money without necessarily being a miser. The loss nearly drove me out of my mind. In a flash I could see all the fresh evils I should be exposed to, and poverty was far from being the worst. I knew my Manon; experience had already taught me all too clearly that, however attached to me she might be when things went well, it was no use counting on her in hard times. She was too fond of wealth and pleasure to give them up for me. I knew that once again I should lose her and everything I loved, and this certain knowledge so tortured me that for some time I played with the thought of putting an end to all my woes by death.

However, I kept enough presence of mind to think out first of all whether I had any resources left, and a comforting idea came to my mind, which was that I might not find it impossible to conceal our loss from Manon while by skill or good fortune I found enough to keep her from want. I consoled myself by recalling that I had calculated that twenty thousand écus would keep us for ten years. Now, I thought, supposing the ten years had gone by without any of the family changes I had hoped for. What should I have done? I am not at all sure, but what is there to prevent my doing now whatever I should have done in those circumstances? How many people are there in Paris at this moment who have neither my wits nor my natural advantages, but who manage to make a living by their talents, such as they are? Thereupon I fell to musing on the ups and downs of life and came to the conclusion that Providence had arranged things pretty wisely, for the majority of the rich are fools – that much is clear to anybody with some slight knowledge of the world. Which proves the ultimate justice of things, for, if they had brains as well as riches, they would be too happy and the rest of men too wretched. The poor are vouchsafed qualities of mind and body to raise them out of their poverty. Some get a share of the wealth of the great by pandering to their pleasures and swindling them. Others try to teach them to be useful citizens – usually, it is true, without success – but that is not the object of divine wisdom; they draw a dividend from their labours by living at the expense of those they instruct, and, from whatever angle you look at it, the stupidity of the rich and great is an excellent source of revenue for the poor and humble.

These reflections put a little heart back in me and cleared my mind. I decided to begin by consulting Lescaut, Manon's brother. He knew his Paris inside out, and it had been all too clearly borne in on me that his main source of income could be neither his property nor his army pay. All I had left was about twenty pistoles that fortunately I had in my pocket. I showed him my purse, described my mishap and my fears, and asked him if there was any choice open to me apart from dying of hunger or taking my own life. He answered that suicide was the last resort of fools, and, as for dying of hunger, plenty of clever people found themselves in that predicament if they were not prepared to use their wits. It was up to me to find out what I was capable of, and I could count on his advice and help in anything I undertook.

'That all sounds rather vague, Monsieur Lescaut,' I said. 'My troubles require a more immediate remedy. For instance, what do you expect me to say to Manon?'

'Manon! why worry about her? Surely with her you have always got the means to end your worries whenever you like? A girl like her ought to be able to keep all three of us.' This outrageous suggestion brought a sharp reply to my lips, but he gave me no time to make it, going on to the effect that he could guarantee a thousand écus to share out between us before the day was out. If I would be advised by him, he knew of a noble lord who was so liberal where his pleasures were concerned that he felt sure he would think nothing of a thousand écus for the favours of a girl like Manon.

At last I managed to stop him. 'I thought better of you. I imagined that the motives behind your friendship were quite the reverse of those you are showing me now.' He impudently admitted that he had always thought the same way himself, but that once his sister had broken the laws of her sex – albeit with the man he liked best in the world – he had only made his peace with her in the hope of making a bit out of her misconduct.

It was easy to see that so far he had been using us for his own ends, but I needed his help so desperately that I stifled any anger I felt and answered laughingly that his suggestion was a last resource that we must not use unless all else failed. Was there any other way open to me?

He next proposed that I should make capital out of my own youth and good looks, and make up to some elderly party who was free with her money. I did not fancy this method either, for it would have meant infidelity to Manon. I mentioned gambling as the easiest way and one more in keeping with my position. He said yes, there certainly was gambling, but that that would have to be gone into very carefully: just plain gambling, with the ordinary chances, was the surest way to ruin. To attempt to practise the little tricks that a skilled player uses to help on his luck was much too risky if you were alone and unsupported. There was a third way, and that was to go into a syndicate, but he was afraid that confederates would think me too young and green to have the skill necessary for joint operations. All the same he promised to put in a word for me, and, to my surprise, he offered to give me some money if I found myself short. The only favour I asked of him, in the circumstances, was to say nothing to Manon about my loss or our conversation.

When I left him I was even less happy in my mind than before, and I was already uneasy about having let him into my secret. He had done nothing for me that I could not have done just as well for myself without having confided in him, and I was mortally afraid he would break his promise to say nothing to Manon. What I had heard of his sentiments gave me grounds for fearing that he would decide to make something out of her (to use his own expression), by taking her out of my hands, or at any rate advising her to leave me and take some richer lover who might prove luckier. The thought plunged me once again into the same nagging despair that I had been in that morning. More than once I was on the point of sending my father a letter full of feigned contrition in the hope of extracting money from him, but I remembered each time that with all his kindness he had shut me up for six months for my first escapade, and I was sure that he would deal much more harshly with me after the sensation my flight from Saint-Sulpice must have caused. Out of this welter of ideas one finally emerged which suddenly brought some sort of calm back to my mind, and I was surprised not to have thought of it before. Why not fall back on my friend Tiberge, in whom I was always sure to find the same unstinting affection? The confidence with which we go to people of tried and tested probity is the best tribute to virtue I know. We feel that no risk is being run. If they are not always in a position to offer practical help, they can at least be relied on for kindness and understanding. As a flower needs only the soft warmth of the sun to make it open out, so the human heart, so tightly closed against all other men, naturally opens in such people's presence.

I interpreted this timely recollection of Tiberge as a sign of heavenly intervention, and I resolved to find a way of seeing him that very day. I went straight back home and wrote him a note suggesting a suitable meeting-place and enjoining absolute secrecy as the most important thing he could do for me in my present circumstances. Fortunately my joy at the prospect of seeing him again smoothed away from my face the traces of worry Manon could not have failed to notice. I referred to our Chaillot mishap as a mere bagatelle not to be taken at all seriously, and, as she enjoyed being in Paris better than anywhere else in the world, she was not sorry to hear me say that we had better stay there until the slight damage caused at Chaillot by the fire had been put right. An hour later I had word from Tiberge promising to keep the appointment. Although I felt a little ashamed at showing myself to a friend whose very presence was a reproach to my excesses, I went there with all speed, keeping my courage up by my knowledge of his kindness of heart and my concern for Manon's interests.

I HAD asked him to be in the garden of the Palais-Royal. He was there first. As soon as he saw me he came forward with outstretched arms and embraced me long and tenderly. He was so deeply moved that I could feel his tears on my cheek. I told him how embarrassed I was at seeing him and how full of a keen sense of my ingratitude, and implored him to tell me first of all whether I could still look upon him as my friend after I had so richly deserved to lose all his respect and affection. He answered in the kindest way that nothing could possibly make him give up such a title, that my very misfortunes and, if he might say so, my sins and excesses had only served to redouble his friendship. But, he added, what he was feeling was the kind of love, mingled with bitter grief, that one feels while helplessly witnessing a dear friend moving speedily towards his doom.

We sat down on a seat.

'My dear Tiberge,' I said with a deep sigh, 'how boundless your pity must be if, as you assure me, it is equal to my woes. I am ashamed to let you see them as they really are, for I admit that they spring from a source that is anything but noble. But the outcome of it all is so deplorable that you could not fail to be touched even if you did not love me as you do.'

He asked me, as a proof of friendship, to tell him frankly everything that had happened since I left Saint-Sulpice. I did so, and far from toning down the truth in any way or minimizing my misdeeds so as to make them sound more excusable, I talked about my passion with all the vehemence it inspired in me. I represented it as one of those peculiar blows, against which virtue is defenceless and wisdom cannot be forearmed, which Destiny aims at some poor wretch when she is bent on his

42

destruction.⌉ I painted a vivid picture of the depths of anxiety, fear and despair I had been in two hours before seeing him, and into which I would assuredly fall back again if my friends abandoned me as heartlessly as Fortune had. In short, I so worked on poor Tiberge's feelings that he was as overcome by compassion as I was by self-pity. He was unwearying in his tender exhortations to cheer up and take heart, but all the time he was assuming that I would have to break with Manon. So I let him see quite clearly that it was this very separation that I looked upon as the greatest of all my misfortunes, and that I was prepared to suffer not only the most abject misery but even the cruellest of deaths before I would accept a remedy more unbearable than all the other ills put together.

'Let us be quite clear, then,' he said; 'what sort of help can I give you if you reject everything I suggest?' I dared not say outright that what I really wanted was his money. But at length he realized this, said that he thought he saw what was in my mind, and then hesitated for some time, obviously wondering what to do. After a pause he said: 'Don't put down my stopping to think this out to any cooling of my friendship or for my desire to help. But think what a quandary you are putting me in! I have either to refuse the only help you are willing to accept, or violate my sense of duty by giving it to you. For shall I not be sharing in your debaucheries if I enable you to persist in them?' He paused again for thought and then went on, 'But perhaps poverty has upset the balance of your mind and not left you free to choose the right path; you cannot appreciate wisdom and truth unless your mind is at peace. I will find a way to let you have some money, but,' he embraced me once again as he said this, 'you must let me make one stipulation. It is that you will let me know where you are living and allow me at least to do what I can to bring you back to virtue. I know you really want to live the good life. It is only the violence of your passions that is holding you back.' I fell in with all his wishes freely and sincerely, and asked him to try to understand the unhappy fate which was making me respond so grudgingly to the advice of such a good friend. He took me at once to a banker he knew, who advanced me a hundred pistoles against a promissory note signed by him. I have already said that Tiberge was not rich, and the last thing he had was ready money. His living was worth a thousand écus, but as that was his first year he had so far received nothing in cash and was making me this loan out of his expectations.

I appreciated the full value of his generosity and was touched by it to the point of deploring the blind passion which was driving me on to dishonour my obligations. For those few minutes virtue found enough strength to rise up within me and combat my infatuation, and in that moment of illumination at least I perceived the fetters of shame and degradation that were binding me. The contest, however, was but a skirmish, and short-lived at that. The mere sight of Manon would have sufficed to make me leap down from Heaven itself, and indeed, when I found myself with her again I wondered how I could for a single moment have been ashamed of such a natural feeling for so bewitching a creature.

Manon had a most extraordinary character. No woman was ever less attached to money for its own sake, and yet she could not for a moment endure the risk of being without it. She had to have pleasures and amusements, but she would never have wanted a sou if enjoyment could have been had free of charge. So long as the day could be spent in pleasure she never troubled her head where the money came from; and so as she was not particularly addicted to gambling, nor dazzled by the mere display of wealth, it was the easiest thing in the world to satisfy her by supplying from day to day the sort of amusements she liked. But this ceaseless round of pleasures was so essential to her being, that without it there was no relying on what she might feel or do. Although she loved me tenderly, and I was the only one, as she was the first to admit, with whom she could taste the full pleasure of love, yet I was almost sure her love would never stand firm against certain kinds of anxiety. Had I had even a modest fortune she would have preferred me to anyone in the

44

world, but I had not the slightest doubt that she would throw me over for some new B. the moment I had nothing to offer her but constancy and fidelity.

With all this in mind I resolved to limit my personal expenditure so rigorously that I could always provide for hers, and to give up a multitude of necessities rather than deprive her even of superfluities. What worried me more than anything else was the upkeep of a carriage, for I could not see how to maintain horses and a coachman. I mentioned my perplexity to M. Lescaut (from whom I had not concealed my having had a hundred pistoles from a friend); and once again he said that if I wanted to try my hand at gaming he did not think it impossible that, provided I were willing to invest a hundred francs or so and treat his friends to a dinner, I might be admitted on his recommendation to the fraternity.[10] I swallowed the distaste I had for swindling, and let myself be carried along by cruel necessity.

That very evening M. Lescaut introduced me as a relation of his, explaining that I was all the more likely to succeed because I was in urgent need of a stroke of good luck. But to make it clear that my poverty was not as abject as all that, he announced that I wished to entertain them to supper. The invitation was accepted and I feasted them royally. For a considerable time the conversation ran along the lines of my handsome appearance and natural gifts. It was asserted that great things might be hoped from me because there was something about my face which suggested the honest man, and nobody would think of expecting anything crooked from me. In fine, a vote of thanks was passed to M. Lescaut for having brought along such a promising novice to the brotherhood, and one of their number was detailed to give me a few days of necessary instruction. The principal scene of my exploits was to be the Hôtel de Transylvanie, where there was a faro table in one room and various card and dice games in the gallery. This institution was run for the benefit of the Prince of R., who was then living at Clagny, and most of his officers belonged to our circle.[11] I must confess to my shame that in a very short time I assimilated all my instructor's lessons. I became particularly adept at turning a card over, and at palming. With the help of a long pair of cuffs I could whisk a card away nimbly enough to deceive the sharpest eye and neatly ruin many an honest player. This amazing skill built up my fortune so rapidly that in a few weeks I found myself possessed of a considerable sum over and above what I shared out loyally with my associates. Gone were all my fears about telling Manon of our loss at Chaillot, and to console her when I broke the sad news, I took a furnished house where we installed ourselves with every appearance of wealth and security.

All through this period Tiberge was regular in his visits and untiring in his moralizings. Day after day he pointed out the wrong I was doing to my conscience, honour and prospects. I put up with his advice good-humouredly, though without the slightest intention of following it, and I was even grateful because I knew it came from the heart. Sometimes I chaffed him about it, even in front of Manon, and recommended him not to be more scrupulous than many a bishop and other ecclesiastic, who contrived to reconcile a mistress and a living. 'Just take a look,' I would say, pointing to my mistress's eyes, 'and say whether there are any sins in the world that are not justified by such a beautiful cause.' He kept his temper; indeed, he was very long-suffering, but when he saw my wealth rapidly increasing, and that I had not only refunded his hundred pistoles but also taken a new house and doubled my expenses, and moreover that I was plunging deeper than ever into dissipation, he completely changed his manner and tactics, denounced my hardness of heart and threatened me with the wrath of Heaven, prophesying some of the evils which speedily overtook me. 'I cannot believe,' he said, 'that all this money you are spending on riotous living has been legitimately come by. You have acquired it by criminal means, and it will be taken away from you in the same way. The most terrible punishment God could inflict on you would be to let you enjoy it in peace. All my advice has been useless and I can see full well that it will soon be resented. So it is good-bye to a weak and thankless friend. May your guilty pleasures vanish like a shadow! May your fortune perish utterly, leaving you naked and alone to learn the vanity of these worldly possessions with which you in your folly are so intoxicated! And when that day comes you will find me ready with my love and help, but from now on I sever all connexion with you, for I detest the life you are living.' This apostolic harangue was delivered in my room and in front of Manon. He got up to go. My instinct was to hold him back, but I was checked by Manon, who said he was out of his mind and the sooner we let him go the better.

And yet these words of his left an impression on my mind. I am careful, you see, to point out the various occasions when I felt an impulse to return to the path of virtue, because such recollections were to be a source of strength to me in some of the most unhappy moments of my life. But at the time Manon's kisses dispelled all my gloom in an instant, and we went on with our life of love and pleasure. Our affection multiplied with our riches, and Venus and Fortune could not have had two more contented slaves. Why, oh why call this world a vale of tears when it is full of such fascinating delights? But alas, the weakness of such delights is that they pass so soon. If only they were made to last, what other joys could man desire? Ours had the common fate: they did not endure and were followed by bitter regrets. I had amassed such profits from gaming that I thought about investing some of my money. My servants were fully aware of my gains, especially my valet and Manon's maid, in front of whom we often talked quite freely. The maid was pretty and the valet in love with her; they had young and easy-going employers to deal with, and they thought they could deceive us without difficulty. They worked out a plan and carried it out with such devastating results for us that they brought us down to a level from which we were never able to rise again.

One day Lescaut had invited us to supper and we returned home at about midnight. I called for my valet and Manon for her maid. Neither came. We were told that they had not been seen in the house for eight hours, and that they had gone off after having had some packing-cases dispatched – by my orders, so

47

they said. I guessed part of the truth, but my worst suspicions were nothing like as bad as the sight I saw when I looked into my room. The lock of my closet had been forced and my money had gone, together with all my clothes. As I was trying to gather my wits together Manon came in, pale with fright, and said that the same thing had been done in her room. The shock was so terrible that it was only by a supreme effort of reason that I prevented myself from giving way to tears and wailing. But, for fear of communicating my despair to Manon, I put on a calm exterior and even told her flippantly that I would get my own back out of some poor dupe at the Hôtel de Transylvanie. But I could see that she was so well aware of our plight that she succeeded far more in upsetting me by her sadness than I did in keeping up her spirits by my feigned cheerfulness. 'We are finished,' she said, with tears in her eyes. I tried vainly to console her with caresses, but my own tears betrayed my consternation and despair. The truth was that we were so completely ruined that we had not a stitch left.

 The best thing seemed to be to send at once for M. Lescaut. He advised me to go without delay to the Lieutenant of Police and Grand Provost of Paris. I went, but it only served to complete my undoing. This step, and those I got the police to take on my behalf, gained me nothing, and by going out I gave Lescaut time to talk to his sister and put a horrible idea into her head. He told her about M. de G. M., an old voluptuary famous for his liberality where his pleasures were concerned, and he let her see so many advantages in being kept by this man that in her troubled state of mind she entered into everything he liked to suggest. This honourable bargain was concluded before I returned, and the execution of it fixed for the next day, after Lescaut had prepared M. de G. M. When I got back I found him waiting for me, but Manon had retired to her room, having given orders for me to be told that she needed rest and quiet and asked me to leave her alone that night. Lescaut offered me a little money, which I accepted, and then he left. It was nearly four in the morning when I went to bed, and then I lay awake for hours turning over ways of recovering my money. Eventually I went to sleep, but so late that I did not wake up until nearly noon. I got up at once to go and see how Manon was, but was told that she had gone out an hour before with her brother, who had called for her in a cab. Such an outing with Lescaut sounded most mysterious to me, but I stifled my suspicions and whiled away some hours in reading. But my uneasiness finally gained the mastery, and I fell to striding up and down our rooms. In Manon's room my eyes fell on a sealed letter on her table. It was addressed to me, in her hand. I shuddered as I opened it. This is what she had written:

> *I swear that you are the idol of my heart, my dear Chevalier, and there is nobody else in the world I love as I love you. But don't you see, my poor darling, that loyalty is a silly virtue in the pass we are in? Do you really think we can love each other with nothing to eat? One fine day hunger would lead me into some fatal mistake, and thinking I was sighing for love I should really be drawing my last breath. I love you, do believe me, but try to leave our affairs in my hands for a little while. Woe betide whoever falls into my clutches; I am out to make my dearest Chevalier rich and happy. My brother will tell you that I cried bitterly at having to leave you, and from him you will be able to have news of – your own Manon.*

I could never describe the state I was in when I had read this letter, and to this day I cannot decide what sort of emotions swirled round in my soul. It was one of those unique situations, the like of which has never been experienced before: you cannot explain to others because they have no conception of what is meant, and you cannot unravel them for yourself because, being unique, they have no connexion with anything in your memory, nor even with any known feeling at all. And yet, whatever my emotions were, certain it is that grief, rage, jealousy, and humiliation all had a share in them. How I wish that love had not had an even greater share! 'She loves me,' I reflected, 'yes, I suppose she does, but after all, what an unnatural monster she would have to be to hate me! Could it be possible to have a better right to anybody's love than I have to hers? Is there anything else I could do for her after all I have sacrificed? And yet she casts me

[handwritten: realizes great distance in breeding + manners -]

off and thinks she can clear herself of all blame simply by saying that she still loves me! She is afraid of hunger – good God! what a coarse, materialistic outlook, and what a response to all my delicacy! Hunger has no terrors for me; I have faced it willingly for her by giving up my fortune and the comforts of my father's home. I have given up necessities so as to satisfy her merest whims and caprices. She loves me, she says! If she did, I know whose advice the wanton creature would have taken; she would not have left me without even saying good-bye. I am the one to talk about the cruel pains of separation, not she! Anyone who deliberately brings such torments upon himself must be out of his mind.'

I was interrupted in these recriminations by an unexpected visitor – Lescaut. As soon as I saw him I put hand to sword. 'You unspeakable wretch!' I said, 'where is Manon? what have you done with her?' He answered nervously that if this was how I welcomed him, just when he was going to tell me about the best thing he had ever done for me, he would go away and never set foot in my house again. I ran to the door, shut it carefully and turned to face him. 'Don't imagine you can take me in again with your fairy-tales,' I shouted, 'defend yourself, or help me find Manon.' 'Now, now, don't you be so hasty,' he said, 'that is the very thing I have come for. I have come to give you some good news you aren't expecting, and I hope you'll show a little gratitude for it.'

I demanded to be told at once, and he spun me a yarn about how Manon had been unable to face the prospect of poverty, and still less that of having to cut down our household all of a sudden, and so had asked him to introduce her to M. de G. M., who had a reputation for generosity. He took good care not to say that the idea had first come from him and that he had prepared the way before taking her to the old man's house. 'I took her there this morning,' he said, 'and the gentleman was so taken with her that he began by inviting her to go and spend a few days with him at his country house. Now I saw at once how you could get something out of this, and I gave him to understand, in a tactful sort of way, that Manon had lost a good deal of money. I managed to tickle up his generosity to the tune of two hundred pistoles, which he gave her as a present to begin with. I said that that was very kind of him for the time being, but that the future would bring many calls on my sister's money as she had undertaken to look after a young brother who had been on our hands since our parents' death. If he thought Manon worthy of his interest (I went on), he would not like to see her suffer on account of this poor lad whom she thought of as part of herself. This story touched his heart, and no mistake. He has promised to rent a nice house for you and Manon, for you are the poor little orphan brother. What's more, to fit you out with decent furniture and pay you four hundred livres a month in hard cash – that is, if my arithmetic is correct, four thousand eight hundred by the end of each year. Before leaving for the country, he gave orders to his steward to find a house and have it ready for his return. And then you will see Manon again. She told me to give you a thousand kisses for her and to say she loves you more than ever.'

I sank on to a seat and mused on this strange twist of fortune. My feelings were so divided and I was in such a state of bewilderment that I went on sitting there without making any answer to the questions Lescaut fired at me one after the other. At that moment honour and virtue once again stung me with remorse, and my thoughts turned wistfully towards Amiens, home, Saint-Sulpice and all the places I had lived in as a clean, self-respecting being. What an immense gulf lay between me and that happy state! It now seemed like some far-off dream, still clear enough to fill me with wishes and regrets, but too vague and misty to stir me to action. What fatal power had dragged me down to crime? How came it that love, an innocent passion, had turned for me into the source of all misery and vice? Who prevented my living peacefully and innocently with Manon? Why had I not married her before claiming anything from her love? If I had really urged a reasonable claim, surely my father would have consented, if only for love of me? He would have loved her as a dear daughter and held her most worthy to be his son's wife. And I should now be happy with Manon's love, my father's affection, the respect of all decent people, Fortune would be smiling on me and I should be virtuous and at peace with myself. What a contrast with the vile part I was now being expected to play! What! did they expect me to share ... But then how could I hesitate since Manon had arranged things this way, since, but for this complaisance, I should lose her altogether? I closed my eyes, as though to prevent my seeing such horrible thoughts, and almost shouted my answer: 'Monsieur Lescaut, I suppose you meant to help me, and I must thank you. You might have found some less unsavoury way, but we'll call it settled, shall we? It only remains for us to think out how best to take advantage of your kindness and fulfil your promise.'

My anger, and the long silence that had followed, had somewhat embarrassed Lescaut, and he was delighted to see me come to a quite different decision from the one he had feared, for he was anything but courageous, as I was to learn in due course. 'Yes, yes,' he said hurriedly, 'I have done you a very good turn, and you will see that we shall make more out of it than you expect.' We proceeded to work out a way of lulling any suspicions M. de G. M. might entertain about our relationship when he saw how much bigger and older I was than he imagined. The only way we could think of was for me to act the simple country bumpkin in front of him and to give him to understand that I was going in for the priesthood and that I went to college every day. To this end we arranged that I should be very shabbily dressed the first time I had the honour of meeting him.

He returned to town three or four days later, bringing Manon to the house that the steward had prepared. She at once let Lescaut know that she was back; he told me, and together we went to see her. Her aged beau had already left.

I had submitted to Manon's will with resigned obedience, but when I saw her again I could not restrain some stirrings of anger within. My joy at seeing her could not altogether overcome my resentment of her infidelity, and I appeared listless and preoccupied. I could not help sighing and uttering such words as 'perfidious' and 'faithless', but she, on the contrary, seemed overjoyed at seeing me again and scolded me for my coolness.

At first she teased me for what she called my greenness, but when she saw how serious I looked, and how hard I was finding it to accept a state of affairs so distasteful to my character and wishes, she went off to her room. I followed her a moment later and found her in tears. When I asked her the reason she said: 'It's perfectly easy to see why. How do you expect me to go on existing if the very sight of me makes you look so gloomy and pained? You have been here a whole hour and not given me so much as a single kiss, and you have accepted mine with all the condescension of the Grand Turk in his harem.'

'Listen, Manon,' I said, taking her in my arms, 'it's no use pretending that I am not cut to the heart, for I am. I am not referring now to the shock your unexpected flight gave me, nor to your cruelty in leaving me without one word of comfort after spending the night in another bed than mine. All that and much more besides would be charmed away by your mere presence. But do you suppose I can contemplate the miserable, degrading life you want me to live in this house without being upset even to the point of tears?' I was weeping myself by now. 'Let us leave my honour and station in life out of this,' I went on; 'little things like that have long ceased to have power to compete with a love like mine. But can't you see that it is this very love of mine that is groaning at being so ill rewarded, or rather so brutally ill-treated by a callous and ungrateful mistress?'

She cut me short. 'Now look here, my dear,' she said; 'what is the use of tormenting me with reproaches that can only break my heart, coming as they do from you? I can see what is upsetting you. I had hoped that you would fall in with the plan I made for recovering some of our lost fortune, and if I had begun to put the plan into effect without your having a say in it, it was simply out of respect for the delicacy of your feelings. But since you disapprove I shall just throw it up!' She added that all she asked was a little forbearance on my part for the rest of that day; she had already had two hundred pistoles from her old gentleman, and he had promised to bring her that night a handsome pearl necklace and other jewels, together with half the year's allowance he had settled on her. 'Only give me time to get his presents into my hands,' she said, 'and I swear he will never be able to boast of any other benefit from the hold I have given him over me, for up to now I have managed to put him off until I am in town. Of course, he has kissed my hands more than a million times, and it is only right that he should pay for the pleasure. I don't think the price of five or six thousand francs is too high when you take into account his money – and his age.'

This decision of hers pleased me much more than the prospect of the five thousand livres. I had not yet lost every honourable feeling, it seemed to me, since I was so glad to be spared this infamy. But I was born to fleeting joys and lasting sufferings. Fate rescued me from one abyss only to hurl me down into another. I showed my gratitude for this change of plan by embracing Manon passionately, and then said that we must inform M. Lescaut so that the three of us could act together. He demurred at first, but the four or five thousand in hard cash brought him cheerfully round to our point of view. It was settled that we should all be present at supper with M. de G. M., and for two reasons: firstly for the fun of the comic turn I was to put on as Manon's student brother, and secondly to prevent the old rake from making too free with his mistress on the strength of having paid liberally in advance. It was arranged that Lescaut and I would take our leave when he went up to the room where he proposed to spend the night, and instead of following him Manon promised to come out and spend it with me. Lescaut undertook to have a carriage waiting at the proper moment outside the door.

Supper-time came, and with it M. de G. M. – Lescaut was there in the room with his sister. By way of an introductory compliment the old chap presented his lady love with a necklace, bracelets and ear-rings, all of pearls and worth at least a thousand écus. Next he counted out two thousand four hundred livres in gold – half the agreed annual allowance. He seasoned his gifts with many graceful attentions in the style of the last reign. Manon could scarcely refuse him a few kisses, if only by way of establishing as many claims on the money he was giving her. All this time I was behind the door, listening for the cue to be given me by Lescaut.

When Manon had put away the money and jewels Lescaut came over, took me by the hand, led me up to M. de G. M. and ordered me to make my bow. I made two or three, of the most obsequious I could. 'Excuse him, Sir,' said Lescaut; 'as you can see he is quite inexperienced and far from having Parisian manners, but we hope that with a little practice he will soon pick things up. You (turning towards me) will often have the honour of seeing this gentleman here, and it is up to you to benefit by such a distinguished example.' The old lover seemed pleased to see me. He tapped me once or twice on the cheek, and told me I must be on my guard in Paris, for young people could easily fall into bad habits there. Lescaut assured him that I was so pious that I was always talking of becoming a priest, and that my greatest hobby was making little chapels. 'I can see something of Manon in him,' said the old man, chucking me under the chin. I answered in a silly voice: 'Sir, you see we two are one flesh, and I love my sister like a second self.' 'There, now!' he said to Lescaut, 'isn't he clever! It's a pity this young man hasn't seen a little more of the world.' 'Oh, Sir,' I went on, 'I have seen plenty of folk in the churches at home, and I think I shall find lots of people in Paris who are not as clever as I am.' 'Fancy!' said he, 'isn't he bright for a country lad!' All through supper the conversation was on about the same level. Manon, who was in a gay mood, nearly upset everything several times by shrieking with laughter. I contrived to tell him his own story, not excluding the nasty dénouement in store for him. It was amusing to see Manon and Lescaut trembling, especially while I was doing a lifelike impersonation of him, but he was too vain to recognize himself, and I brought the story to so neat a conclusion that he was the first to find it vastly amusing. You will see in due course that I have my reasons for dwelling on this ridiculous episode. At length bedtime drew near, and he began saying things about the impatience of lovers. Lescaut and I withdrew. He was helped up to his room, and Manon, alleging a natural need, slipped away and joined us at the front door. The carriage was waiting three or four doors down the street, and it came to pick us up. In a trice we were far away.

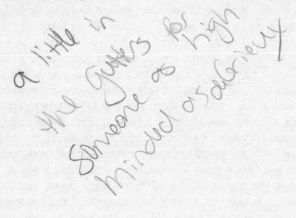

a little in the gutters for high someone as high minded as Gabriel

ALTHOUGH I realized that this action was a real piece of roguery, it was not what lay most heavily on my conscience. I had far more scruples about the money I had made at the gambling-table. And yet we did not get the benefit of either, and Heaven ordained that the more venial of these crimes was to have the heavier punishment.

M. de G. M. soon found out that he had been tricked. I do not know whether he took steps that very night to have us tracked down, but his influence was powerful enough to make any steps he took immediately effective, while we were rash enough to count far too much on the size of Paris and the distance between our neighbourhood and his. Not only did he quickly find out our address and our real position, but also who I was, the life I had been leading in Paris, the story of Manon's former liaison with B. and the way she had swindled him too — in fact all the scandalous details of our past. He made up his mind to have us arrested and treated less as criminals than as out-and-out immoral characters. We were still in bed when a police officer entered, followed by half a dozen guards. Their first act was to seize our money, or rather that of M. de G. M.; then they hauled us brutally out of bed and took us outside where two vehicles were waiting; poor Manon was unceremoniously bundled into one, and in the other I was taken off to Saint-Lazare. Nobody who has not been through such vicissitudes can conceive into what depths of despair they can throw you. The loutish guards would not even allow me to kiss Manon good-bye or say a single word to her. For a long time I had no idea what had become of her, which was perhaps as well for me in the first few days, for such a catastrophe might have cost me my reason, not to say my life.

My unhappy mistress had been taken off and put into an

institution which I cannot name without horror.[12] What a fate for the most beautiful of women, who, if all men had my eyes and heart, might have sat on the most exalted throne in the world! She was not roughly treated, but confined alone in a narrow prison and condemned to perform some menial task every day as a necessary condition for obtaining some revolting food. All this I learned only long afterwards, when I myself had undergone several months of cruel and monotonous punishment. As the guards had not told me where they had orders to take me, I found out my destination only at the very gates of Saint-Lazare. I had such terrible ideas about this place that at that moment I would have preferred death to the fate I believed to be in store for me.[13] My fears were redoubled at the entrance, when the guards went through my pockets for the second time to make sure that I had no weapons or means of defence. My arrival was reported to the Father Superior, who came at once and greeted me very kindly. 'Father,' I said, 'no humiliations, please. I would rather die.' 'No, no, Sir,' he said, 'if you behave reasonably we shall get along quite well with each other.' He bade me follow him to an upper room, and I meekly obeyed. The soldiers came with us as far as the door, and then the Superior discharged them and came in with me.

'So I am your prisoner,' I said. 'Well, Father, what do you propose to do with me?' He said he was very pleased to see me take such a reasonable line and that his duty was to strive to inspire in me a taste for virtue and religion, whilst mine was to mark well his exhortations and advice. If only I would try to respond to kindness I would find my confinement quite enjoyable. 'Enjoyable!' I said. 'You do not know the only thing in the world I could enjoy.' 'Yes I do,' he said, 'but I hope your inclinations will change.' I gathered from this reply that he was aware of my story and probably of my name, and I begged him to say if this was so. He answered, of course, that he had been told everything.

This was the rudest shock of all. I could not get over the

humiliation of being the talk of all my acquaintances and the shame of the family. At first I wept bitterly, in violent convulsions of despair, and then for a whole week was cast down into the deepest apathy, with no ear or thought for anything but my disgrace. Even thoughts of Manon lost their power to add to my grief, but receded into the background of my mind, where they lurked as the memory of an earlier pain. My heart was filled with shame and confusion which dominated every other emotion.

Few can know the full power of these afflictions of the soul. Most men are touched only by five or six passions, and their whole life, with all its storms and stresses, moves round within this circle. Take away love and hatred, pleasure and sorrow, hope and fear, and there is nothing else they feel. But characters of a more delicate texture can be tossed about in a hundred different ways; they seem to have more than five senses, and to be a prey to ideas and sensations surpassing the ordinary limits of nature. And being conscious of this refinement which raises them above the ordinary run of men, they cherish this sensibility of theirs more jealously than anything else. That is why scorn or laughter tortures and exasperates them, that is why shame is one of their most violent emotions.

This sorry distinction was mine at Saint-Lazare. My grief seemed so excessive to the Superior that he felt obliged to treat me with great gentleness and indulgence, for fear of what I might do. He came and saw me two or three times a day, and often took me for walks round the garden. On these walks he never tired of reasoning with me and offering me sound advice. I listened with great docility and even expressed my gratitude, and he took this as an earnest of my approaching conversion. 'You have such a good and gentle disposition,' he said one day, 'that I cannot comprehend the excesses you are accused of. Two things astonish me: one is how, with all your great qualities, you can have given yourself over to such dissipation, and the other, which I find even more difficult to understand, is how you heed my advice and instruction so meekly after living for several years

in habitual vice. If it is repentance, you are a signal example of
the mercy of God; if it is natural goodness, at least it means that
your character is unimpaired, and that leads me to hope that we
shall not need to hold you here for long before we can bring you
back to a sane and balanced life.' I was delighted that he had
such a good opinion of me, and I resolved to cultivate his esteem
by behaviour which would completely satisfy him, in the belief
that it would be the surest way of shortening my imprisonment.
I asked for some books. He left me a free choice of what I
wanted to read, and was surprised that I selected serious authors.
I pretended to study them with the utmost concentration, and on
every occasion I gave him evidence of the change of heart he
wished to see.

All this, of course, was purely external. To my shame it must
be said that at Saint-Lazare I played the perfect hypocrite. When
I was unobserved, instead of studying I did nothing but rail
against my destiny, and curse my prison and the tyranny that
kept me there. No sooner did I feel some relief from the overwhelming sense of humiliation than I was seized anew by the
torments of love. All I could think of was my absent Manon, my
uncertainty of her whereabouts and my fear of never seeing her
again. I pictured her in the arms of M. de G. M. – that was the
first thought I had – for, far from imagining that he had dealt
out to her the same treatment as he had to me, I felt sure that he
had had me put out of the way simply in order to possess her in
peace.

And so the seemingly eternal days and nights dragged on, and
my only hope lay in the effect of my hypocrisy on the Superior. I
carefully studied his words and the expressions on his face so as
to find out what he thought of me, and as he was the arbiter of
my fate I spared no effort to please him. It was easy to see that I
was in his good books and I was sure that he could be relied
upon to do his best for me.

One day I made so bold as to ask him whether my liberation
depended on him. He said that his powers did not quite extend
to that, but that his report would, he hoped, persuade M. de

G. M., at whose request I had been imprisoned, to restore me my freedom. 'Dare I hope,' I said in honeyed tones, 'that he will think the two months' imprisonment I have already served are a sufficient expiation?' He promised to speak to him about it if I wished, and I most earnestly begged him to do me this kindness.

Two days later he told me that G. M. had been so touched by the good report he had had of me that not only did he seem disposed to set me free,.but had also shown a strong desire to know me better and intended to visit me. Although I could scarcely look forward to seeing him, I interpreted this visit as a further step towards liberty.

In due course he came to Saint-Lazare. He looked more dignified and less foolish than when I had seen him in Manon's house. He made a few edifying remarks about my misconduct, and added, apparently to justify his own goings-on, that it was permissible for men in their frailty to gratify certain of nature's demands, but that swindling and scoundrelly trickery ought to be punished. He seemed pleased by the meekness with which I listened. I did not even take offence when he allowed himself a few jokes about my supposed family relationship with Lescaut and Manon, and the little chapels of which, he presumed, I must have made quite a number at Saint-Lazare, since I found so much enjoyment in that pious occupation. But, unfortunately for him and for me, he let slip a remark that no doubt Manon too must have made some pretty ones in the Hôpital. This word gave me a shock, but I kept enough self-control to ask him to be so good as to explain. 'Why, yes,' he said, 'for the past two months she had been learning wisdom at the Hôpital, and I trust she has benefited there as much as you have at Saint-Lazare.'

Even if at that moment I had been faced with imprisonment for life or death itself, I could not have restrained my fury at this terrible news. I flung myself upon him with such uncontrollable rage that I had only half my real strength, but I still had enough left to throw him on to the floor and seize him by the throat. I had half strangled him when the sound of his fall and the shrill cries he managed to utter, in spite of my grip on his throat, brought in the Superior and several monks, who set him free. By this time I too was at the end of my tether and gasping for breath. 'Oh God!' I cried, almost choking with sobs, 'oh God of justice, how can I ever survive so foul an insult?' I tried to throw myself afresh upon this monster who had outraged me, but was held back. You cannot imagine how I shouted and wept in my anguish, and my behaviour was so frenzied that the others, not knowing the reason, looked at each other with as much alarm as amazement. Meanwhile M. de G. M. was adjusting his wig and cravat, and in his fury at having been so roughly handled he ordered the Superior to confine me more closely than ever, using all the punishments known at Saint-Lazare. 'No, Sir,' said the Superior, 'we cannot treat a person of the Chevalier's rank in such a manner. Besides, he is so gentle and well-behaved that I find it difficult to believe that he has gone to such lengths without strong provocation.' This answer put the finishing touch to M. de G. M.'s discomfiture, and he went out vowing to find a way of crushing the Superior, me and anybody else who dared to stand up to him.

The Superior ordered his monks to show him out. When he was left alone with me he begged me to explain at once the cause of this disturbance. 'Oh, Father,' I said, still weeping like a child, 'think of the most loathsome cruelty, the most inhuman savagery you can imagine, and that may give you some inkling of what this unspeakable G. M. has done. He has dealt me a blow from which I shall never recover. I should like to tell you the whole story. You are kind and you will have pity on me.' I gave him a short account of my long and unconquerable passion for Manon, our flourishing position before we had been robbed by our own servants, the offer made to my mistress by G. M., the conclusion of their bargain and the way it had been broken. True, I put things in the most favourable light from our point of view. 'And that,' I continued, 'is what lies behind M. de G. M.'s zeal for my conversion. He was in a position to have me shut up in here out of pure spite. I could forgive that, but that is not all. The woman I hold more precious than my own life has been brutally carried off by his orders and put ignominiously into the Hôpital – he had the impertinence to tell me so himself this very day. The Hôpital, Father! My beautiful Manon, my own beloved, thrown into that place like the filthiest harlot! Shall I ever find strength to live through the grief and shame of it all?' Seeing me in such depths of affliction, the worthy priest tried to console me, saying that he had never known the true facts of my story as I had just put them. He had known, of course, about my disorderly life, but he had supposed that the motives behind M. de G. M.'s action had been concern for me and family friendship. That was the only interpretation he had been able to find, and what I had just told him put a very different complexion on the affair. He felt sure that the true account he now intended giving to the Lieutenant-General of Police would hasten the day when I should be set free. He then asked me why I had not yet thought of letting my family know what had become of me; since they were not responsible for my captivity. I met this objection with reasons drawn from the grief I had been afraid of inflicting on my father, and the shame I should have felt myself. He finally promised to go at once to the Lieutenant-General if only to forestall some still more sinister move on the part of M. de G. M., who had gone off in an ugly mood and who was influential enough to be dangerous.

I waited for his return with all the apprehension of a poor wretch whose sentence is about to be pronounced. It was an indescribable torture to imagine Manon at the Hôpital. Apart from the disgrace of her being there at all, there was my ignorance of what sort of treatment she was receiving, while recollections of the few details I had heard about that horrible place constantly revived my anxieties. I was so determined to help her, at any cost and by any means, that I would have set fire to Saint-Lazare if it had not been possible to get out by any other method. And so I pondered over the ways open to me if the Lieutenant-General of Police persisted in keeping me there by force. I cudgelled my brains and explored every possibility, but I could find nothing that would guarantee a certain escape, and was afraid of having the watch on me tightened still more if I made an unsuccessful attempt. I went over the names of friends from whom I might expect assistance, but how could I let them know about my predicament? In the end I thought I had settled on a plan so skilful that it could hardly fail, and I decided to postpone improving on it until the Father Superior's return and the fruitlessness of his errand had made it necessary.

He soon came back, and his expression bore none of the signs of joy that one associates with good news. 'I have spoken to the Lieutenant-General,' he said, 'but I was too late. M. de G. M. went to him straight from here and has so prejudiced him against you that he was on the point of sending me fresh orders to confine you more closely. Yet when I told him the full details of your story, he seemed much more favourably disposed, smiled at old M. de G. M.'s lecherousness and said that you would have to be left here six months to pacify him. And it would be all to the good,' he added, 'since this place could not do you any harm. He enjoined me to treat you well, and I assure you that you will have nothing to complain of from me.'

This explanation lasted long enough for me to make the prudent reflection that if I showed too much enthusiasm for my freedom I might risk upsetting all my plans. I therefore affirmed that as I had to stay there in any case, it would be a great consolation for me to know that I had some small share in his affection. Then, without appearing to attach too much importance to it, I asked him to do me a favour which would greatly contribute to my peace of mind; it was to notify a friend of mine, a priest at Saint-Sulpice, that I was at Saint-Lazare, and to allow him to visit me from time to time. He granted this without hesitation.

I was thinking of Tiberge. Not that I hoped he would help to set me free, but I meant to use him indirectly to that end, without his even being aware of it. This, in a word, was my scheme: I proposed to write to Lescaut and get him and our friends to liberate me, but the first difficulty was to have a letter delivered into his hands, and that was where Tiberge came in.

But then, as Tiberge knew that he was my mistress's brother, he might be reluctant to undertake such a task. My idea was to enclose a letter to Lescaut inside another addressed to a perfectly respectable acquaintance, with a request that it be sent on promptly. It was essential to see Lescaut so that we could agree on a plan of action, and I purposed instructing him to come to Saint-Lazare in the guise of an elder brother of mine who had come to Paris especially to find out how things stood with me. I would wait until I saw him before settling on the safest and quickest way of escape.

The Father Superior had Tiberge informed of my wish to see him. That loyal friend had not lost touch with me to the extent of not knowing what had become of me; he knew I was in Saint-Lazare, and possibly he was not altogether sorry to know about my disgrace, for he thought it might bring me back to a sense of duty. He came with all speed.

We talked in the friendliest way. He wanted to know just what my position was. I hid nothing from him except my intention to escape. 'My dear friend,' I said, 'you are not the sort of man before whom I want to appear what I am not. If you think you have come here to see a reformed character, with passions all under control, a libertine whose eyes have been opened by the chastisement of God, in a word a heart purged of desire and no longer ensnared by Manon's wiles, you have judged me too indulgently. You see me now just as you left me four months ago, still susceptible, still haunted by that fatal passion, still untiringly seeking happiness there and there alone.'

He replied that such an admission made my conduct unpardonable. Many a sinner was so intoxicated with the treacherous joys of evil that he openly preferred them to virtue, but such a man was at any rate lured on by appearances of happiness, even though spurious. But to see clearly, as I did, that the object which held me in its toils could only make me wicked and unhappy, and to persist, nevertheless, in plunging into misery and crime, was a contradiction between knowledge and behaviour which did little credit to my good sense.

'Tiberge,' I said, 'how easy it is for you to carry the day with nothing to withstand your attacks! But let me have a turn at arguing. Can you assert that what you call the happiness of virtue is free from pain, disappointments and anxieties? How would you describe the prisons, crosses, tortures and executions inflicted by tyrants? Would you say, like the mystics, that what torments the body is bliss to the soul? You would never dare, the paradox is indefensible. No, this happiness you rank so high is mixed with countless sufferings, or rather it is a tissue of ills through which felicity may possibly be discerned. Now if by sheer imagination men can find pleasure in these very ills on the grounds that they may lead to some ultimate and hoped-for joy, why do you dismiss an exactly similar line of conduct on my part as contradictory and senseless? I love Manon; I am striving through a thousand ills towards a goal of peace and happiness with her. The path I am treading is hard, but it is softened by my hope of reaching the goal, and I shall deem all the cares on the way more than repaid by one moment with her. So things seem about equal on your side and on mine. If there is a difference it is still in my favour, for the bliss I hope for is near, and yours is far off; mine is of the same nature as the sorrow, that is to say corporal, whilst yours is of an unknown kind which faith alone can substantiate.'

This argument horrified Tiberge. He recoiled from me, saying in the most solemn way that not only were my words an affront to common sense, but that they were a heinous sophism born of impiety and irreligion, for it was a most monstrous and godless thing to make such a comparison between the goal of my sufferings and that of religion.

'I grant you,' I replied, 'that it is not a fair comparison, but take note that my argument does not depend on that. I simply wanted to explain what you call a contradiction in my perseverance in an unhappy love, and I think I have satisfactorily proved that, if contradiction there be, you cannot avoid falling into it any more than I can. That is the only sense in which I treated the things as equal, and I still maintain that they are. You will no doubt answer that the aim of virtue is infinitely higher than that of love. Who would gainsay that? But is that the point at issue? Aren't we discussing the power of each of these things to enable us to bear sufferings? They must be judged by results. How many people desert the cause of strict virtue, but how few forsake that of love! Or again, perhaps you will answer that if there are difficulties in the good life they are not inevitable and necessary, that tyrants and tortures are no longer the rule and that many virtuous people nowadays lead a tranquil and happy life. But in the same way I can say that love often runs a peaceful and untroubled course, but with this difference that is most advantageous to my argument. Love, I must add, though it may often deceive us, does at least promise only satisfaction and pleasure, whereas religion expects us to be prepared for a life of gloom and mortification.' Seeing signs of righteous anger on his part I went on: 'Don't be alarmed; the only conclusion I want to draw from this is that, if you want to cure a lovesick heart, the worst method you can adopt is to decry the joys of love and promise greater happiness in the exercise of virtue. Being made as we are, it is indisputable that our felicity is found in pleasure, and I challenge anyone to define it in any other way. Now the human heart does not need prolonged study to feel that of all pleasures those of love are sweetest, and it very soon perceives that a promise of greater joys elsewhere is a fraud, and a fraud which predisposes it to mistrust the most solemn assurances. Let the preachers who seek to lead me back to virtue say by all means that virtue is necessary and indispensable, but they must not hide the fact that it is austere and painful. Let them establish that the delights of love are ephemeral, forbidden and liable to be followed by eternal punishment, and, what might make a still stronger impression on me, that the more sweet and captivating they are the more magnanimously Heaven will reward such a great sacrifice. But they must allow that with hearts like ours we cannot find more perfect joys here below.'

Tiberge was somewhat cheered by this conclusion to my discourse, and admitted that there was some sense in my opinions.

His only other objection was to ask why I did not follow out my own principles by sacrificing my present love for the prospect of a reward which I valued so highly. 'My dear fellow,' I answered, 'This is where I admit my unworthiness and lack of strength. Ah yes, duty says I should practise what I preach, but am I capable of any action at all? Think of the help I should need to make me forget Manon's charms!' 'God forgive me,' said Tiberge, 'this sounds like some more of this Jansenist fatalism.' 'I don't know what I am,' I answered, 'and I am not at all sure what I ought to be, but I am experiencing all too clearly the truth of what the Jansenists say.'

This conversation had at least the one useful result of reviving my friend's sympathy. He realized that my misdeeds were due not so much to perversity as to weakness, and this made his friendly soul more ready to help me later on when without him I should assuredly have perished of misery and want. But I did not give him the slightest hint of my intention to escape from Saint-Lazare. I merely asked him to undertake to deliver my letter, which I had got ready before he came. I easily found reasons for having had to write it, and he was loyal enough to carry out my instructions exactly. Before the end of the day Lescaut received the note addressed to him.

THE next day he succeeded in getting through to see me by passing himself off as my brother. I was overjoyed at seeing him safely in my room, and shut the door carefully. 'There is not a moment to lose,' I said. 'First tell me what news of Manon, and then how to get out of here.' He explained that he had not seen his sister since the day before I was imprisoned, that he had found out her fate and mine only by dint of careful investigation. He had presented himself two or three times at the Hôpital, but had not been allowed to speak to her. 'Curses on G. M.!' I cried. 'He'll pay dearly for this!'

'Now about setting you free,' said Lescaut. 'This is not such an easy job as you think. Two of my friends and I spent all yesterday evening looking at the outside of the building and we came to the conclusion that it would be very difficult to get you out, with your windows looking on to a courtyard surrounded by bricks and mortar, as you yourself told me. What's more, you are on the third floor and we can't bring in any ladders or ropes. So I can't see any chance from the outside. Something will have to be worked out for an inside job.' 'No,' I said, 'I have looked into everything, especially since I have not been watched so closely, thanks to being in the Superior's good books. They no longer lock my door, and I am free to walk about in the monks' galleries, but all the staircases are cut off by heavy doors that are kept shut night and day. There is no way of getting out by mere skill.' I paused to think things out, and an excellent notion came to my mind – or it seemed so to me. 'Just a minute!' I said. 'Could you bring me a pistol?' 'Quite simple,' said Lescaut, 'but you don't want to kill somebody, do you?' I assured him that so far from my wanting to kill anybody I did not even mind whether

69

the pistol was loaded or not. 'Bring it tomorrow,' I said, 'and don't fail to be opposite the main entrance at eleven o'clock at night, with two or three friends.' I hope to be able to join you there.' He did his best to make me tell him some more, but in vain. I said that the enterprise I had in mind was of the sort that could seem feasible only after it had succeeded. I then asked him to cut his visit short so as to have no trouble about being admitted the next day. He was allowed in with as little trouble as the first time. He wore a very dignified look, and nobody would have taken him for anything but an honourable man.

When I found myself possessed of the instrument that was to gain me my freedom, I had scarcely any doubt left that my scheme was going to come off successfully. It was a strange and daring one, but with such motives as mine I felt that there was nothing I could not do. Since I had been allowed to leave my room and walk about in the galleries, I had noticed that every evening the janitor took the keys of all doors to the Superior, and that after that everybody went to bed and a deep silence reigned throughout the building. There was nothing to prevent my passing from my room to his through the communicating gallery. My object was to get the keys from the Superior by threatening him with the pistol if he showed signs of refusing, after which I would use them to gain the street. I impatiently waited for the time to come. The janitor did his rounds at the usual time, soon after nine. I let another hour go by so as to be sure that all the monks and servants were asleep, and then I set out with my weapon and a lighted candle. I knocked softly on the Superior's door so as to wake him without a lot of noise. He heard me the second time I knocked, and rose from bed and opened the door, probably thinking that one of the monks was unwell and in need of help. But he first took the precaution of calling through the door to ask who it was and what I wanted. I had to say my name, but I put on a plaintive tone to suggest that I felt ill. Then he opened the door and said: 'Ah! my dear son, is it you? What brings you here so late?' I went in, and drawing him to the far end of the room made it clear to him that I could not stay any longer in Saint-Lazare, that night-time was best for getting out unobserved and that I asked him, as a friendly act, to be so kind as to open the doors or to lend me the keys so that I could open them myself.

This polite speech must have astonished him. He looked me up and down for some time without saying a word. As I had no time to lose I went on to say that I had been most touched by his kindness, but that liberty being the most precious of all possessions, especially for one unjustly deprived of it, I was determined to get it that night and at any price. For fear he might take it into his head to raise his voice and call for help I let him see the very convincing argument for silence that I had under my jacket. 'A pistol!' he said. 'What, my son, do you mean to show your gratitude for my kindness to you by taking my life?' 'God forbid!' I answered. 'You have too much intelligence to put me to that necessity; but I mean to be free, and I am so set on it that if my plan miscarries because of you, it's all up with you.' 'But, my dear son,' said he, pale and trembling, 'what harm have I done you, what reason have you for desiring my death?' 'No, no,' I answered impatiently, 'I have no intention of killing you if you want to live. Simply open that door, and I shall be your best friend.' I noticed the keys on the table, took them and requested him to follow me and make as little noise as possible.

He had to resign himself to it. Each time he opened a door as we went along he said with a sigh, 'Ah, my son! Ah, who would ever have believed it?' And each time I replied, 'Not so much noise, Father.' At length we reached a sort of barrier just short of the main entrance. I already felt free, and was standing behind the reverend father with the candle in one hand and my pistol in the other. While he was busying himself with the door the sound of the bolts being shot back awoke a servant who slept in the adjoining room. He got up and poked his head out of the door. Apparently the worthy priest thought this fellow could stop me, for he rashly ordered him to come to his aid. He was a powerful man and without hesitating he made one leap at me. I did not stop to argue with him, but fired point blank into his chest.

'There, that is your doing, Father,' I said, not without pride, 'but that is no reason for not finishing the job.' I pushed him to the last door, which he dared not refuse to open, and I stepped gaily out and found Lescaut waiting a few yards away, with two friends as he had promised. We made off.

Lescaut asked me if he had not heard a pistol-shot. 'Yes, it's your fault,' I said. 'What did you bring me a loaded pistol for?' But all the same I thanked him for having taken this precaution, but for which I should certainly have been at Saint-Lazare for a long time. We went for the night to a tavern where I made up somewhat for the meagre fare I had had for nearly three months. But I could not really enjoy myself, for in my mind I was sharing Manon's cruel sufferings. 'She must be set free,' I said to the three others; 'it was for that alone that I wanted to get free myself. I want you to lend me your brains – for my own part I am ready to give my life.'

Lescaut, who was both intelligent and cautious, pointed out that I must hasten slowly, for my escape from Saint-Lazare, and in particular the mishap I had had on the way out, would certainly cause a sensation, the chief of police would hunt me out, and his arm was long. In fact, unless I was anxious to court something worse than Saint-Lazare, I should be well advised to lie low and stay indoors for a few days until the initial fury of my enemies had had time to die down. This was wise counsel, but it needed a wise man to follow it. All this delay and circumspection accorded ill with my passion, and the furthest I would go was to promise to spend the next day in bed. He shut me in his room, where I stayed until evening.

I spent part of this time turning over ways and means of rescuing Manon. One certain thing, I felt, was that her prison was even more impenetrable than mine had been. Force or violence would be unavailing, some sort of trickery would be needed; but the goddess of invention herself would not have known where to begin. I could see so little daylight that I put off going into it more carefully until after I had found out something about the internal arrangements of the place.

As soon as nightfall came and it was safe for me to go out, I asked Lescaut to accompany me. We struck up a conversation with one of the doorkeepers who seemed a sensible fellow. I palmed myself off as a stranger who had heard very good opinions expressed about the Hôpital and the excellent way it was run. I questioned him on the minutest details, the talk led on to the board of governors, and I asked him to tell me their names and something about their personal circumstances. The answers under this second heading put an idea into my head which I at once thought a very good one and set to work to put into practice. I asked him (it was a most important part of my plan) whether any of these gentlemen had children, and was told that he could not give me a full list, but that he knew M. de T., one of the principal governors, had a son of marriageable age who had often visited the institution with his father. This information was good enough for me.

I broke off the conversation as soon as I could and on the way back told Lescaut the scheme I had thought of. 'I am assuming,' I said, 'that M. de T. the younger, being rich and well connected, is no more averse from a little pleasure than most young fellows of his age. He cannot be a woman-hater, nor so absurd as to refuse his help in an affair of the heart. I propose to interest him in Manon's freedom. If he is a man of feeling and a gentleman he will help us out of the kindness of his heart. If he cannot be influenced by that motive he will at any rate do something for a pretty girl, if only in the hope of having a share in her favours. I mean to see him, and I don't want to put it off any longer than tomorrow. The project has cheered me up so much that I think it must be a good omen.'

Lescaut agreed that there was something in it and we might hope for results from this course. I was not so miserable that night.

Next morning I dressed as smartly as my poverty-stricken condition allowed, and took a cab to the house of M. de T. He was surprised at this visit by someone unknown to him, but his expression and politeness struck me as promising. I explained the object of my visit in a straightforward way and appealed to his natural feelings by describing my passion and my mistress's charms as two things beyond comparison except with each other. He said that he had not seen Manon, but had heard of her – at least if she was the one who had been old G. M.'s mistress. I guessed that he would have been told about the part I had played in that affair, and so I decided to win his sympathy by a little praiseworthy candour. I told him the whole story of Manon and myself. 'So you see, Sir,' I concluded, 'that both my life and my heart's desire are now in your hands, and the one is no more precious to me than the other. I am hiding nothing from you because I have been told how generous you are, and the similarity between our ages makes me hope that our inclinations may also have something in common.' This show of frankness and candour seemed to impress him. He answered like a man who knows the world and also has delicacy of mind, a quality the world does not always give but often takes away. He said that he counted my visit as a stroke of good fortune, that he regarded my friendship as one of his most valued acquisitions and that he would strive to deserve it by helping me as energetically as he was able. He did not promise to give me back Manon, for he said that his influence was neither powerful nor infallible, but he did offer to arrange for me to have the pleasure of seeing her, and to do his utmost to restore her to me. This diffidence of his pleased me better than a sweeping promise to fulfil all my wishes, for the very moderation of his offers appealed to me as a sign of honesty. In a word, I confidently expected great things from his good offices. The mere promise to get me an interview with Manon would in itself have made me his devoted servant. I showed him something of what I felt in a way that made him feel on his side that I was not wanting in character. We embraced each other affectionately, and became firm friends out of sheer goodness of heart and that natural impulse which draws a warmhearted and honourable man towards another of the same type.

He expressed his friendship in still more practical form, for having pondered over my adventures and guessed that I could not have been well off when I came out of Saint-Lazare, he offered me his purse and urged me to accept it. I declined, but said, 'No, my dear Sir, you are too good. If through your great kindness and friendly help I succeed in seeing Manon again, I am your servant for life. If you restore her to me altogether, I shall think that my debt to you can never be repaid even if I shed all my blood for you.'

Before we separated we agreed on the time and place of our next meeting. He was kind enough not to keep me waiting longer than the afternoon of the same day.

At about four o'clock he joined me in a café, and together we set out for the Hôpital. As we made our way through the court-yards I was trembling at the knees. 'Oh, all-powerful god of love,' I said, 'so I am to see once again the idol of my heart, the object of so many tears and anxieties! Vouchsafe me life to reach her side, only that, and thereafter do as you will with my fortune and my life. I have no other boon to ask.'

M. de T. had a word with various warders who were only too willing to do anything they could to please him. He had the block pointed out where Manon's room was, and the attendant who took us had a gigantic key which opened the door. This man was also the one detailed to look after her, and on the way I asked him how she had spent her time. He said that she was as gentle as an angel; he had never had a hard word from her. For six weeks after her arrival she had done nothing but weep, but for some time now she seemed to be bearing her troubles more patiently, and spent all her day from morning till night sewing, apart from an hour or two set aside for reading. I renewed my inquiries whether she had been properly looked after, and he assured me that at any rate she had never lacked necessities.

As we drew near her door my heart was beating furiously. I said to M. de T., 'You go in alone and prepare her for my coming, for I fear that she will be too overcome if she sees me all of a sudden.' The door was opened. I stayed in the passage, but overheard their conversation. He said that he was one of my friends and very concerned for our happiness, and that he had come to bring her a little comforting news. She begged him most urgently to say whether he could tell her what had become of me. He promised to bring me kneeling at her feet, still as loving and devoted as she could wish. 'When?' she said. 'Now, this very day,' he answered. 'The long wished-for moment is coming. He will be here now, if you want him.' She realized that I was at the door, and was rushing there as I entered and caught her in my arms. We clung to each other with all the outpouring of tenderness true lovers find so sweet after three months of separation. For a quarter of an hour M. de T. beheld a touching scene composed of sighs, half-stifled exclamations and a thousand loving names murmured softly to each other. 'I envy you,' he said at length, making us sit down; 'there is no career of glory I would not give up for such a beautiful and loving mistress.' 'And I would scorn all the empires of the world,' I answered, 'for the joy of knowing I was loved by her.'

Needless to say, all the rest of the conversation we had so longed for was filled with infinite tenderness. Poor Manon told me her story and I told her mine. The pitiful state she was in and the privations from which I had just emerged moved us both to bitter tears. M. de T. consoled us with renewed promises to devote himself unstintingly to bringing about an end to our woes. He advised us not to spin this first interview out to too great a length so that he could more easily arrange others for us. But he found it very hard to make us see the point of this advice. Manon found it especially difficult to make up her mind to let me go; she continually held on to my hands and clothes, pushing me back on my chair and saying, 'What a place to leave me in! How do I know I shall ever see you again?' M. de T. promised to come frequently and to bring me with him. 'And as to this place,' he added with a smile, 'we must not call it the Hôpital any more. Since a person worthy to reign over all hearts has been kept here, it is Versailles!'

As we went out I gave a generous tip to the attendant to encourage him to do his best for her. The man was less mercenary and hard-hearted than such fellows usually are. He had been present at our meeting and had been touched by our love, and the gold piece with which I presented him won him over completely. On the way down to the courtyards he took me to one side and said, 'Sir, if you will take me into your service or give me some suitable compensation for the loss of my job here, I think I could easily set Mademoiselle Manon free for you.' I listened to his proposal and promised him things far beyond his desires, although I was penniless myself, for I relied on finding some easy way of rewarding a man of his stamp. 'Take it from me, my friend,' I said, 'that there is nothing I will not do for you, and your future is as safe as mine.' I wanted to know what means he intended to employ. 'Why,' he said, 'simply to unlock her door one evening and escort her as far as the street, where you must be ready to meet her.' I asked whether there was any fear of her being recognized in the passages and courtyards. He admitted that there was some danger of that, but said that there were some risks that had to be taken.

His keenness delighted me, but I called in M. de T. to lay the project before him, together with the only drawback which might make it unsafe. He saw more difficulties than I had. He agreed that it was quite possible that she might get away by such means, but he pointed out that if she were recognized and stopped while attempting to escape it might be all up with her for good. 'Moreover,' he went on, 'you would have to leave Paris at once, for you would never be sufficiently hidden from a search. The search would be intensified for you as well as for her, and while one man alone can easily dodge his pursuers, it is next to impossible to remain unobserved in the company of a pretty woman.' This argument, however well-founded it might seem, could not carry any weight in my mind against an immediate prospect of setting Manon free. I said so to M. de T., begging him to be indulgent towards a lover's imprudence and rashness. I added that I certainly did mean to leave Paris and put up in some nearby village as I had done before. So we settled with the attendant that our attempt should not be put off any later than the morrow, and, to make assurance as sure as in us lay, we decided to smuggle in men's clothes to simplify the escape. It was not easy to get the clothes into her room, but my resourcefulness was not at a loss for a way. I merely asked M. de T. to wear two thin waistcoats, one over the other, when he came next day, and I undertook to see to the rest.

When we went back on the following day I had with me underclothes, stockings, etc. for Manon, and was wearing a long cloak over my jacket to hide any bulges in my pockets. We stayed only a minute in her room; M. de T. left her one of his waistcoats and I gave her my jacket, trusting to the cloak to get me safely out. She thus had a complete outfit – except the breeches, which I had unfortunately overlooked.

We might have had a good laugh at the absence of this vital garment if it had not put us into so serious a predicament. As it was, I was in despair at our being held up by such a silly little thing. However, there was only one thing to be done, and that was for me to leave my own breeches for Manon and get out somehow without them. My cloak was very long, and thanks to the help of a pin here and there I was fit to pass through the door with the decencies preserved. When at last night had fallen, after a day that seemed interminable to me, we took a carriage to a position just down the street from the door of the Hôpital. We had not long to wait before we saw Manon appear with her guide. We had the door open and they both jumped in at once. My dearest Manon sank into my arms. She was trembling like a leaf. The driver asked us where he was to go. 'To the end of the world!' I cried. 'Anywhere you like, so long as I am never parted again from Manon!'

This involuntary flourish nearly landed me in a nasty mess. The coachman noticed my language, and when I went on to tell him the name of the street to which we wanted to be taken, he answered that he was afraid I was letting him in for some shady business; that it was plain to see that this pretty young man, whose name was Manon, was a girl I was smuggling out of the Hôpital; that he was not feeling in the mood to get himself into trouble for love of me. This fellow's scruples were merely a desire to make me pay more for the carriage. We were too near the Hôpital not to go warily. 'Be quiet!' I said. 'There's a louis for the earning.' After that he would have helped me burn down the Hôpital itself. We reached the house where Lescaut lodged, but as it was late we dropped M. de T. on the way, with promises to meet next day. The attendant stayed with us.

I was holding Manon so tightly in my arms that the two of us took up only one seat. She was weeping for joy and I could feel her tears on my face. When we had to alight at Lescaut's lodgings I had a fresh altercation with the driver which was to have a disastrous sequel. I regretted having promised him a louis, not only because it was an absurd sum, but for another and much better reason which was that I was not in a position to pay. I sent for Lescaut who came down from his room, and I told him in a whisper what a fix I was in. He was an outspoken man and not at all given to humouring coachmen, and he said I must be joking. 'A gold louis!' he said. 'Twenty strokes with a stick for a rogue like that would be more like it!' I tried in vain to point out in an undertone that he would be our undoing; he snatched my stick out of my hand and made as if to go for the cabby. The man, who most likely knew by experience what it was like to fall into the hands of a Lifeguardsman or Musketeer, fled in terror with his cab, shouting that I had swindled him and would hear from him again. Once more I shouted to him to stop, but to no purpose. I was most uneasy at his having run off in this way, for I was sure he would go to the police. 'You are putting me in a terrible position,' I said to Lescaut. 'I shall not be safe here; we shall have to clear off at once.' I gave Manon my arm to help her along, and we hurried away from that dangerous street, Lescaut and all.

THERE is something uncanny about the way in which Provi- dence links one event to another. We had been walking for five or six minutes at the most, when a man, whose face I could not see, recognized Lescaut. No doubt he was looking for him round about his lodgings with the fell purpose he now carried out. 'You're Lescaut!' he said. 'Tonight you'll be having supper with the angels!' He fired a pistol at him and at once made off. Lescaut fell lifeless. I urged Manon to fly, for we were useless to a corpse, and I was afraid of being arrested by the watch who were bound to come on the scene. With her and the attendant I darted down the first narrow turning. She was so panic-stricken that I could hardly prevent her from collapsing. At last I saw a cab at the end of the street. We jumped in. But when the driver asked us the address I was nonplussed, for I had no safe retreat, no trusty friend I dared fall back on, and no money either, having barely half a pistole left in my purse. Manon was so unhinged by terror and fatigue that she was only half conscious and slumped down by my side. Moreover, my own thoughts were haunted by the murder of Lescaut and I was still nervous about the watch. What was to be done? Happily I remembered the inn at Chaillot where I had spent some time with Manon when we had first gone to that village to look for somewhere to live. I hoped to find safety there, and, what was more, to be able to live there for a while without having to pay. So I ordered the driver to take us to Chaillot. He refused to go as far as that so late at night for less than a pistole. Another awkward moment. Eventually we agreed on six francs – all I had left in my purse.

On the journey, for all my attempts to console Manon, I had death in my heart. Had I not had in my arms the only thing which bound me to this world, I would have taken my own life, and this consideration alone restored some calm to my mind. 'I love her, she loves me, she is mine,' I said to myself. 'Tiberge can say what he likes. This is no empty shadow of happiness. I would see all the rest of the world perish and not care a rap. Why? Because I have no love left for anything else.' There was some truth in the sentiment; but, all the same, at that moment when I was so lightly dismissing this world's possessions I felt that I could have done with just a small share of them, if only so as to be able to scorn the rest more loftily. Love is stronger than wealth, mightier than treasures and riches, but it can do with their help; and nothing is more exasperating to a delicate-minded lover than to see himself brought, willy-nilly, down to the level of coarser souls simply through lack of money.

It was eleven o'clock when we reached Chaillot. They welcomed us at the inn like old friends, and were not surprised to see Manon in male attire, for it is quite common in and around Paris to see women in all sorts of disguises. I ordered everything to be done for her just as though I were at the height of opulence. She did not know that my purse was so poorly, and I took care not to let her know, having decided to go back to Paris alone next day to seek some remedy for this tiresome complaint.

At supper I saw how much paler and thinner she was. I had not noticed it at the Hôpital because the lighting in the room where I had seen her was not of the best. I asked her whether this pallor was still the effect of the shock of seeing her brother murdered. She declared that, although she was very upset by the accident, her paleness was due solely to her having been parted from me for two or three months. 'You really love me very much?' I said. 'A thousand times more than I can say,' she replied. 'You will never leave me again?' 'No, never.' And this vow was sealed by so many oaths and caresses that I felt it impossible that she could ever forget. I had always been convinced that at the moment she meant what she said, for what reason could she have had for play-acting to that extent? But she was even more fickle than sincere; or rather, when she was in poverty and need and saw other women living in luxury, she ceased to have any fixed character at all, and did not even recognize herself. I was about to have a final proof of this, a proof more conclusive than all the others, and one which has led to the strangest adventure ever to befall a man of my birth and position.

As I was aware of this side of her character I hurried off to Paris next day. Her brother's death and the urgent need of getting clothes and a change of linen for herself and me were such good reasons that I did not have to look for excuses. As I went out I said to Manon and the host that I was going to take a cab, but that was mere bravado. Sheer necessity obliged me to go on foot, and I walked with all speed as far as the Cours-la-Reine, where I intended to stop for a moment of peace and quiet in order to think things out and decide what I was going to do in Paris.

I sat down on the grass and launched into a sea of reasoning and arguments which gradually sorted themselves out under three main headings: I needed immediate financial help for countless pressing necessities; I had to find some means of living which would at any rate lead to hopes of future security, and, last but not least, I had to see how the land lay and take steps to guarantee Manon's personal safety and my own. After having gone through all the plans and calculations I could think of under these three heads, I decided that after all I had better cut out the last two. We were fairly well hidden in our room at Chaillot, and it seemed time enough to think of future needs when I had satisfied the present ones.

So the real point was to refill my purse at once. M. de T. had kindly offered me his, but I was most reluctant to have to raise the point with him. What a part to have to play – that of displaying one's poverty to a stranger and begging him to share his money with one! Only a craven little soul, so devoid of feeling that he could not see the humiliation of it, would be capable of such a thing: or else a Christian, whose real humanity and greatness of soul raised him above such diffidence. I was neither one thing nor the other, and I would have given half my blood to be spared this indignity.

'Then there is Tiberge,' I thought. 'Surely my good Tiberge will not refuse anything he can give me? No, my plight will touch his heart, but his moral sermons will be the death of me. I shall have to swallow his reproaches, exhortations and threats; he will exact such a price for his help that there again I would give part of my blood rather than have to face a tiresome scene which will leave me all upset and plagued with remorse. Very well, then, I shall have to give up all hope, since there is no alternative left and I am so averse from stopping to consider these, that I would rather shed half my blood than have recourse to either – that is to say the whole of my blood rather than try both. Yes, the whole of my blood,' I reflected; 'I would cheerfully shed it all rather than stoop to grovelling supplications.

'But what has my blood got to do with it? What matters is Manon's life and how to keep her alive; all that matters is her love, her loyalty. Have I anything worthy to be weighed in the balance against her? Such a thought has never occurred to me until now. For me she is glory, happiness and fortune. No doubt there are many things I would give my life to have or to avoid, but to value a thing higher than my life is no reason for valuing it as high as Manon.' After this thought I did not take long to make up my mind. I went on my way, intending to call first on Tiberge and to go on from him to M. de T.

When I reached Paris itself I took a cab, although I had not the wherewithal to pay for it. I relied on the help I was going to ask for. I had myself driven to the Luxembourg, whence I sent a message telling Tiberge that I was waiting for him. He satisfied my impatience by coming at once. I told him of my desperate situation without any beating about the bush. He asked me if the hundred pistoles I had repaid him would do, and without a word of objection he went straight off to get the money, with that look of open-hearted joy in giving only seen in love and true friendship. Although I had never for a moment doubted that my appeal would succeed, I was surprised to have got what I wanted with so little trouble, that is to say without hard words from him on my impenitence. But I made a mistake in thinking that I could get away scot-free and without any criticism, for when he had finished counting out the money, and I was getting ready to leave him, he asked me to take a stroll with him round a path in the park. I had not mentioned Manon's name, and he did not know that she was at large, and so his sermon was concerned only with my escape from Saint-Lazare and his fear that I might relapse into my evil ways instead of profiting by the lessons in wisdom I had been given in prison. He told me that having been to see me at Saint-Lazare on the day after my escape he had been horrified beyond words to learn how I had taken my departure; he had had a talk with the Superior, who had not yet recovered from his shock. The good Father had nevertheless been generous enough to keep the circumstances of my going from the knowledge of the police, and had thus prevented the news of the porter's death from being known outside. I therefore had no grounds for alarm on that score; but if I had any decent feelings left I would learn my lesson from the fortunate turn things had taken, thanks to divine intervention. I ought to begin by writing to my father and seeking a reconciliation; and if, for once, I would listen to his advice, he thought I ought to leave Paris and go back to the bosom of my family.

I heard this speech out to the end. There were several reassuring features about it. First of all I was overjoyed to have nothing more to fear from Saint-Lazare; once again the streets of Paris were a free country for me. Secondly I congratulated myself that Tiberge had no idea that Manon was at liberty and back with me. I did not fail to notice that he had avoided mentioning her name to me, presumably because he thought my apparent calmness about her meant that she was beginning to lose her hold on my affections. I decided, if not to return to my family, at least to write to my father, as Tiberge suggested, and to express my readiness to come back to a sense of duty and obedience. I hoped by this means to cajole some money out of him, on the pretext that I was going to study at the Academy, for I should have been hard put to it to convince him that I was in a frame of mind to take up an ecclesiastical calling again. And, seriously, I was not at all averse from what I was prepared to promise him; on the contrary, I was really looking forward with pleasure to taking up something regular and intellectual, insofar as it would fit in with my love. I reckoned that I could live with Manon and do my studies at the same time. The two things were perfectly compatible! These ideas pleased me so much that I promised Tiberge to send off a letter to my father that very day. When I left him I did in fact go to a public writing-room and wrote such an affectionate and submissive letter that when I read it over I flattered myself that it would coax something out of the paternal heart.

Although I could have taken a cab and paid for it after leaving Tiberge, I took special pleasure in striding boldly along to M. de T.'s and enjoying the liberty which my friend had assured me was no longer in any danger. But suddenly it occurred to me that his reassurances applied only to Saint-Lazare, and that on top of that I had the Hôpital affair on my hands, to say nothing of my being involved, if only as a witness, in the death of Lescaut. This recollection scared me so much that I ran down the first alley I could find and from there hailed a cab. I went straight to M. de T., who laughed at my terror, which seemed laughable to me, too, after he had told me that I had nothing to fear from the Hôpital, nor over the Lescaut affair. He explained that, thinking he might be suspected of having had some part in the abduction of Manon, he had gone to the Hôpital that morning and had asked for her, pretending not to know what had happened. Far from accusing either of us, they had made a point of telling him the extraordinary story; they were amazed that such a pretty girl as Manon should have brought herself to run away with an attendant. He had simply observed in a detached way that he was not at all surprised and that people will stop at nothing in order to get free. He had gone on from there to Lescaut's lodgings, he told me, hoping to find me and my charming mistress there, but the landlord, a coachbuilder by trade, had sworn that he had not set eyes on either of us, adding that it was not surprising that we had not been to his house if it was to see Lescaut, because we must certainly have learned that he had just been killed at about the same time. After that he had not needed pressing to retail all he knew about the cause and circumstances of the murder. About two hours earlier one of Lescaut's friends in the Lifeguards had been to see him and had suggested a game of cards. Lescaut had won so quickly that within an hour his friend had found himself the poorer by a hundred écus, that is to say all his money. The poor devil, now quite penniless, had asked Lescaut to lend him half of what he had lost, and this had led to some haggling which had developed into a most violent quarrel. Lescaut had refused to go and fight it out with swords, and the other had gone off vowing to smash his skull in, which threat he had carried out that very evening. M. de T. was good enough to add that he had been very worried about us, and that his offer of help was still open. I did not hesitate to tell him where we were hiding, and he asked me to allow him to come to supper.

As my only remaining task was to get some linen and clothes for Manon, I said that we could set off at once if he would not mind stopping for a few minutes with me at one or two shops. I do not know whether he thought I was suggesting this with a view to exciting his generosity, or whether it was a spontaneous impulse of his kindly nature; but having agreed to leave at once, he took me to the shops that supplied his own home, made me choose various materials considerably more expensive than I had meant to get, and when I was about to pay, forbade the shopkeepers to accept a penny from me. This graceful gesture was so tactfully made that I felt quite at ease in profiting by it.

Together we made for Chaillot, and when I arrived there I was in a much less worried state of mind than when I had left.

The Chevalier des Grieux had been speaking for over an hour, and I asked him to take a little rest and have some supper with us. He knew that we had enjoyed listening to him because our interest had never flagged, and he promised us that we should find something still more interesting in the sequel to his story. When supper was over he took up the tale again in these words.

PART TWO

My PRESENCE and the polite attentions of M. de T. soon dispelled the last traces of Manon's gloom. 'Dearest love,' I said as I came in, 'let us forget the past and its terrors, let us start a new and happier life than ever. After all, Love is a kind master who gives us more pleasure than all the ills changing fortune could inflict.' Supper was a really festive affair.

With Manon and my hundred pistoles I was prouder and happier than the richest tax-collector in Paris with all his piles of treasure. Wealth should be reckoned by our means to satisfy our desires, and not one of mine was left unfulfilled. Even the future gave me few qualms; I was almost sure that my father would make no difficulty about giving me enough to live on decently in Paris, for as I was now in my twentieth year I should soon have a right to demand my share of my mother's property.[14] I did not hide from Manon that my capital consisted of only a hundred pistoles. It was enough to live on in a small way while waiting for the happier turn of fortune which, I felt, was bound to come either through my own rights of succession or through gaming.

And so for the first few weeks my only concern was to get the most enjoyment I could out of the situation. It was as much my sense of honour as a lingering respect for the police that made me put off from day to day renewing my old relationship with the fraternity at the Hôtel de Transylvanie. I restricted my activities to playing in a few less notorious haunts, where good luck spared me the humiliation of having to resort to sharping. I spent part of each afternoon in town, returning to Chaillot for supper, as often as not with M. de T. whose friendship for us grew more intimate every day.

Manon found ways of combating boredom. With the coming

of spring some of the young ladies had returned to the district, and she struck up an acquaintance with them. They divided their time between little excursions and trivial feminine occupations, and defrayed the cost of the carriage by arranging gambling parties with strictly limited stakes. They used to go and take the air in the Bois de Boulogne, and when I came home in the evenings it was to find Manon happier and more devoted to me than ever.

Yet a few clouds did arise which looked like threatening the stability of my happiness. But they were soon completely dispelled, and Manon's merry humour made the upshot so comical that I can still find wistful pleasure in recollecting an episode typical of her affection and fanciful wit.

One day I was drawn aside by the one and only servant in our establishment, who said, with much embarrassment, that he had an important secret to acquaint me with. I encouraged him to speak freely, and after some beating about the bush he gave me to understand that a foreign gentleman seemed to have developed a passion for Mademoiselle Manon. I felt a cold shudder run through all my veins. 'Does she return it?' I broke in, more sharply than was prudent if I wanted to find out. The violence of my tone unnerved him, and he answered that he had not been able to see into things as deeply as that. He did say, however, that for some days past he had noticed that this stranger was assiduous in his visits to the Bois de Boulogne, and that he had made a habit of leaving his carriage and walking alone among the trees, apparently looking out for a chance to see or meet Mademoiselle. My servant had therefore decided to strike up an acquaintance with the gentleman's servants so as to find out his name. To the best of their knowledge he was an Italian prince, and they suspected that he was up to some amorous intrigue. He added nervously that he had not been able to find out anything else because at that moment the prince had emerged from the wood, come up to him without ceremony and asked him his name, and, as if he guessed he belonged to us, had congratulated him on being in the service of the most charming person in the world.

I impatiently waited for the rest of the tale and he ended up with lame excuses due, I imagined, to my ill-advised display of agitation. In vain did I urge him to go on and keep nothing back; he protested that that was all he knew, and that as what he had told me had happened only the day before he had not seen the prince's servants again. I set his mind at rest, not only by praising him but by giving him a handsome tip into the bargain, and without letting him see that I mistrusted Manon in any way, asked him in a calmer tone to keep an eye on all the stranger's movements.

But all the same his embarrassment left me in agonies of doubt, for it might have made him hold back part of the truth. But when I had thought it over a little I recovered from my panic and regretted having betrayed my weakness in this way. It was no crime on Manon's part that people fell in love with her, and everything seemed to point to her being unaware of the conquest she had made. What sort of a life was I going to lead if I was capable of harbouring jealousy so readily? The next day I went back to Paris without having formed any plan beyond that of increasing my wealth as quickly as possible by playing for higher stakes, so as to be in a position to leave Chaillot at the first sign of trouble. I learned nothing disquieting that evening. The stranger had reappeared in the Bois, and on the strength of what had happened the day before he had again come up to my man and talked about his love, but in terms which did not suggest he had any understanding with Manon. He had questioned him on all sorts of details and finally tried to win him over by lavish promises, and, taking out a letter which he had ready prepared, he had vainly tried to make him accept some gold pieces if he would deliver it to his mistress.

Two days went by without further incident. The third was more stormy. It was rather late when I reached home, and I was told that during her walk Manon had left her friends for a moment: she had made a sign to the stranger, who had been following her at no great distance, and when he had come up to her she had given him a letter which he had received with every appearance of rapture. She had run off at once, only giving him time to express his joy by printing loving kisses on her handwriting. But she had seemed unusually gay for the rest of the day, and this mood had persisted since her return home. I think I shuddered at each word. 'Are you quite sure,' I said sadly to my man, 'that your eyes have not deceived you?' He called on Heaven to witness to his good faith. I do not know to what lengths my tortured heart might have led me, but just then Manon, who had heard me arrive, came out to meet me, looking impatient and scolding me for my slowness. Without waiting for me to speak she smothered me with kisses, and when we were alone she reproached me quite bitterly for the habit I was getting into of coming home so late. Seeing me silent she went on to say that I had not spent a whole day with her for three weeks: she could not endure such long absences and asked me to spare her at least one day now and then. She wanted me to stay with her the very next day from morning till night. 'I shall be there, make no mistake,' I answered sharply. She appeared not to notice my ill humour, but in an outburst of seemingly overwhelming joy she described in full and very amusing detail all that had happened to her that day. 'What a strange woman she is, and what does this prelude betoken?' I thought, remembering the circumstances of our first separation. And yet I was struck by something genuine in her joy and caresses, some inner harmony with the outward appearances.

I could not help feeling gloomy during supper, but it was easy to ascribe that to losses sustained at cards. It had occurred to me that it was most fortunate that the idea of my not leaving Chaillot next day came from her, for it gave me time to think things out. My being at home removed all sorts of fears for the morrow, and if I noticed nothing to make me bring my discoveries out into the open, I had already decided to move the day after that to a part of Paris where there would be no Italian princes to deal with. While this scheme ensured my having a peaceful night's sleep, it did not take away my nagging anxiety about a possible new infidelity.

When I woke up Manon informed me that by spending the day at home she did not mean that she wanted me to look slovenly, and she proposed to dress my hair with her own hands. I had a very fine head of hair and she had often amused herself in this way. But this time she took more care over the task than I had ever known her take before. To satisfy her, I had to sit in front of her dressing-table and submit to every little device she could think of for my embellishment. As she worked she frequently turned my face towards her, put her hands on my shoulders and scrutinized me with hungry eyes; then, expressing her satisfaction with a kiss or two, she would turn me round again and go on.

This dalliance kept us busy until dinner-time. She had seemed so genuinely interested in it, and her gaiety smacked so little of artifice, that I was quite unable to make such apparent devotion tally with any intent to deceive me in so foul a manner. More than once I was tempted to open my heart to her and unburden myself of a load that was beginning to weigh me down, but each moment I flattered myself that the initiative would come from her, and promised myself the delights of a triumph.

We went back into her boudoir, where she began to tie up my hair, and I was indulgently submitting to her every wish when it was announced that the Prince of ***** was asking to see her. This name filled me with fury. 'What!' I cried, pushing her away from me, 'Who? What prince?' She made no answer. 'Show him up,' she coolly said to the servant, and then, turning to me: 'Darling mine, I adore you,' she said in her most bewitching tones. 'I ask you for a moment's indulgence. One moment, only one moment, and then I shall love you a thousand times more, and be grateful all my life.'

I was dumbfounded with surprise and indignation. She repeated her entreaties while I cast round for words with which to throw them back at her with scorn. But hearing the ante-room door open, she grasped my floating hair in one hand, seized her mirror in the other, and exerting all her strength hauled me in that state across the room, pushed the door open with her knee, and presented the stranger, whom the noise had rooted to the middle of the floor, with a sight that must have caused him no little astonishment. I saw a well groomed but exceedingly ugly man.

In spite of his bewilderment, he did not fail to make a deep bow. Manon gave him no time to open his mouth, but thrusting her mirror in his face said: 'Look, Sir. Have a good look at yourself and give me a fair answer. You ask for my love. Here is the man I love and whom I have vowed to love all my life. Compare for yourself. If you think you can compete with him for my heart, pray tell me on what grounds, for I declare that in the eyes of your humble servant all the princes in Italy are not worth one of the hairs I am holding in my hand.'

All through this crazy speech, which had clearly been thought out in advance, I vainly struggled to get free and, taking pity on a man of such position, I was moved to make amends for this petty outrage by saying something civil to him. But he quickly recovered himself, and I gave up my idea on hearing his reply, which struck me as rather crude: 'Mademoiselle, Mademoiselle,' he said, with a forced smile, 'I certainly have had my eyes opened, and I see you are far less of a novice than I had supposed.'

He took himself off at once without giving her another look, muttering that the women of France were no better than those of Italy. And on this occasion there was nothing to make me want to give him a better impression of the fair sex.[15]

Manon let go of my hair, flung herself into an armchair and the room re-echoed with her peals of laughter. I will not deny that I was touched to the heart by a sacrifice which I could ascribe only to love. All the same, the joke seemed to me a trifle overdone, and I criticized her for it. She told me that my rival, having pestered her for several days in the Bois de Boulogne, and having conveyed his feelings by grimacings, had made up his mind to send a formal declaration, together with his name and a full list of his titles, in a letter he had had delivered by the coachman who drove her and her friends. He had promised her a brilliant fortune and eternal adoration away over the mountains.

She had come back to Chaillot intending to tell me the whole story, but, thinking we might get some fun out of it, she had not been able to resist the vision her imagination had conjured up. And so she had sent the Italian prince a flattering reply, giving him free permission to come and see her, and had given herself a second pleasure by making me participate in her plan without having the slightest suspicion. I did not say a word about the information that had reached me through other channels, and in the ecstasy of triumphant love I approved of everything.

I HAVE noticed all through my life that Heaven has always chosen the time when my happiness seemed most firmly established for aiming its cruellest blows at me. I thought I was so happy with Manon's love and the friendship of M. de T. that it would have been impossible to convince me that I had any new disaster to fear. But even then a new one was being prepared so terrible that it reduced me to the state you saw me in at Pacy, and by degrees to such deplorable straits that you will scarcely be able to believe that my story is true.

One day we had M. de T. with us for supper and we heard a carriage draw up at the door. Curiosity made us wish to know who could be arriving at such an hour, and we were told that it was young G. M., that is to say the son of our most implacable enemy, the old profligate who had sent me to Saint-Lazare and Manon to the Hôpital. The name brought the blood rushing to my cheeks. 'Heaven has led him here,' I said, 'to be punished for his father's misdeeds. He will not get away before he has crossed swords with me.' M. de T., who knew him – indeed he was one of his closest friends – tried to induce me to think differently of him, assuring me that he was a very good fellow and so incapable of having had any share in his father's actions that I would not set eyes on him for a moment without feeling respect for him and wanting to have his. He added many other flattering things about him and begged me to let him go and invite him to come and sit at our table and join us for the remainder of our supper. He forestalled the objection that Manon might be exposed to danger if her whereabouts were known to the son of our enemy, by swearing on his faith and honour that when he got to know us we could not have a more zealous champion. After such assurances I made no further demur.

Before bringing him in, M. de T. spent a moment explaining to him who we were. The air with which he came in certainly made a favourable impression upon us. He embraced me. We sat down. He had a word of appreciation for Manon, me and everything that belonged to us, and he ate with a relish that did honour to our meal.

When the table had been cleared, conversation became more serious. As he referred to his father's vindictiveness towards us, he lowered his eyes and made the most abject apologies. 'I pass quickly over all that,' he said, 'so as not to revive a memory which fills me with shame.' If his protestations were sincere from the outset, they became still more so as time went on, for before he had talked in this way for half an hour I noticed the effect Manon's charms were having on him. Gradually his eyes and his manner became more languishing. He did not let anything show in his words, but, without needing any help from jealousy, I had too much experience of love not to be able to discern whatever sprang from that source. He stayed with us well into the night and before leaving said how happy he was to have met us, and asked permission to come again and renew his offers of friendship. He went off early next morning, taking M. de T. with him in his carriage.

As I have said, I did not have any feeling of jealousy, for I accepted Manon's word more implicitly than ever. That lovely creature was so completely mistress of my heart that I harboured no emotions other than respect and love. Far from blaming her for having attracted young G. M., I was most gratified by the power of her charms and congratulated myself on being loved by a woman whom everybody found so lovable. I did not even think there was any point in revealing my suspicions to her. For some days we were busy having her clothes fitted and wondering whether we could go to the theatre without risk of being recognized. M. de T. came to see us before the week was out, and we asked his advice. He realized that he had to say yes to please Manon, and we decided to go that same evening with him.

But this project could not be carried out, for he at once drew me aside, and this is what he said: 'I have been most worried since I saw you, and that is why I have come here today. G. M. is in love with your mistress; he has admitted as much to me. I am his intimate friend, and anxious to do anything for him, but I am just as much yours. I consider his intentions wrong and I have told him so. I would have respected the confidence he placed in me if he had intended to use normal means to gain his end, but he knows all about Manon's character. I cannot say where he has found out, but he certainly has, that she is fond of luxury and pleasure, and as he is already quite well off he has told me that he means to begin by tempting her with some very costly present and the offer of ten thousand livres a year. Other things being equal, I might have been much more reluctant to give him away, but my sense of justice, together with feelings of friendship, have made me do this for you; particularly as, having by my imprudence been the cause of his passion by bringing him here, I am in honour bound to prevent the effects of the evil I have caused.'

I thanked M. de T. for having done me such an important service, and returned his confidence by admitting to him that Manon's character was in fact what G. M. supposed, I mean that she could not bear the word poverty. 'But,' I went on, 'if it is only a question of more money or less, I do not think she is capable of giving me up for another man. I am in a position to give her everything within reason, and I reckon that my resources will grow from day to day. There is only one thing I am afraid of, and that is that G. M. may take advantage of this knowledge of our whereabouts and do us some bad turn.' M. de T. was sure that I need have no anxiety on that score. G. M., he said, was capable of an amorous indiscretion, but not of stooping to a dastardly trick; if he were mean enough to do such a thing, he himself would be the first to punish him and thereby make amends for the wrong he had done me by making it possible. 'I am much obliged to you for such kind words,' I said, 'but by that time the mischief would be done and the remedy would be very questionable. The wisest counsel seems therefore to forestall it by leaving Chaillot and going somewhere else to live.' 'Yes,' said M. de T., 'but you will have your work cut out to do so as quickly as you ought, for G. M. is due here at noon; he told me so yesterday, and that is what has made me come so early to tell you what he has in mind. He may be here any moment.'

The urgency of this warning made me look into the affair more seriously. As it seemed impossible to avoid G. M.'s visit, and it would probably be equally difficult to prevent his opening his heart to Manon, I decided to forewarn her myself of the plans of this new rival. I imagined that if she knew that I was aware of the proposals he was going to make, and if they were made before my eyes, she would find enough courage to turn them down. I let M. de T. see what I had in mind, and his answer was that it was all very delicate. 'Yes, I grant you that,' I said, 'but, if anyone can be sure of such a thing, I certainly have all the grounds for being sure of her affection. The only thing that might dazzle her is the mere size of the bait held out, and I have already told you that she is not interested in money. She likes her comforts, but she also likes me, and in the present state of my finances I cannot believe that she would throw me over for the son of the man who clapped her into the Hôpital.' In short, I persisted in my ideas, drew Manon to one side and told her frankly everything I had just learned.

She thanked me for my good opinion of her and promised to receive G. M.'s offers in a way that would leave him no desire to start them again. 'No, don't do that,' I said, 'you must not upset him by being rude: he might be in a position to be dangerous. But,' I laughingly went on, 'you little hussy, you know all there is to know about getting rid of unpleasant or tiresome lovers.' She pondered for a little while and then said: 'I have thought of a first-rate plan and I am very proud of my ingenuity. G. M. is the son of our most cruel enemy; we must pay out the father, rather than the son, by taking revenge on his purse. I mean to listen to him, accept his presents, and then play him up.' 'It is a pretty idea,' I said, 'but, my poor dear, you forget that was the road which led us straight to the Hôpital.' It was all very well for me to point out the dangers of such a course; she replied that it was merely a matter of setting about it properly, and overrode all my objections. If you can name me one lover who does not blindly subscribe to every whim of the woman he worships, I will admit that it was wrong of me to give in so easily. And so the decision to make a fool of G. M. was taken, and by a strange twist of my destiny it turned out that it was he who made the fool of me.

His coach appeared at about eleven. He made some very well-turned compliments about taking the liberty of coming to dine with us. He was not surprised to find M. de T. there, for he had promised the day before that he would come too, but had pretended to have some business or other so as to avoid having to come in the same carriage. We all sat down with outward signs of confidence and friendship, although there was not one of us who did not harbour treachery in his heart. G. M. found a very easy chance of declaring his sentiments to Manon. I must have seemed very obliging, for I left the table for a few minutes for that express purpose. On my return I noticed that he had not been reduced to despair by any excessive severity. He was in the best of spirits. I made a point of appearing so too; he was laughing inwardly at my gullibility and I at his. All through the afternoon each of us provided a diverting spectacle for the other. Before he left I arranged for him to have a moment of private talk with Manon, so that he had grounds for being as gratified by my complaisance as by my good dinner.

As soon as he had climbed into his carriage with M. de T., Manon rushed at me with outstretched arms, hugged me and gave vent to peals of laughter. She repeated his speeches and suggestions word for word, and they boiled down to this: he adored her, he wanted to share with her the forty thousand livres a year that he already enjoyed, apart from what he expected after his father's death, she was to be mistress of his heart and fortune, and by way of a pledge of his benefactions he was prepared to give her a coach, a furnished house, a maid, three lackeys and a chef. 'Here we have a son very much more generous than his father,' I said. 'Now, honestly, doesn't this offer tempt you just a little?'

'Me?' she answered, and adapted some lines of Racine to fit her idea:

> *Moi! vous me soupçonnez de cette perfidie?*
> *Moi! je pourrais souffrir un visage odieux*
> *Qui rappelle toujours l'Hôpital à mes yeux?*

'No,' I went on, taking up the parody:

> *J'aurais peine à penser que l'Hôpital, madame,*
> *Fût un trait dont l'amour l'eût gravé dans votre âme.**[16]

'but what about a furnished house with a coach and three lackeys? There is something very seductive about that, and Love has few more deadly weapons.' She protested that her heart was mine for ever, and that it would never succumb to any other attacks but mine. 'The promises he has made are a stab demanding vengeance rather than a wound from Cupid's bow,' she said. I asked her whether she intended to accept the house and carriage and she answered that she was only after his money. The difficulty was to get the one without the other. We decided to wait for the full

---

*These lines might be roughly translated:

> *'What me? How can you credit such a thing?*
> *What? feast my eyes on such a hateful face*
> *Which always brings to mind that beastly place?'*

> *'I hardly thought, my dear, that Cupid's dart*
> *Had etched his name and Bridewell on your heart.'*

Eriphile: *Moi? vous me soupçonnez de cette perfidie?*
> *Moi, j'aimerais, madame, un vainqueur furieux,*
> *Qui toujours tout sanglant se présente à mes yeux,*
> *Qui, la flamme à la main, et de meurtres avide,*
> *Mit en cendres Lesbos . . .*

Iphigénie: *Oui, vous l'aimez, perfide!*
> *Et ces mêmes fureurs que vous me dépeignez,*
> *Ces bras que dans le sang vous avez vus baignés,*
> *Ces morts, cette Lesbos, ces cendres, cette flamme,*
> *Sont des traits dont l'amour l'a gravé dans votre âme . . .*

It was very natural that Manon and des Grieux should be able to parody Racine, for they were both theatre-mad.

statement of his projects which G. M. had promised to send in a letter. It was duly delivered the next day by a lackey not in livery who very skilfully found means of speaking to her without witnesses. She told him to wait for the answer, and brought the letter straight to me. We opened it together. Apart from the commonplaces of love-making, it contained my rival's offers in detail. He stopped at no expense, but undertook to hand over ten thousand francs when she took possession of the house, and to make up any depletions of that sum so that she could always have it by her in cash. The day of setting up house was not delayed very long, for he wanted only two days for the preparations, and he gave her the name of the street and of the house where he promised to meet her on the afternoon of the second day, if she could evade my clutches. That was the only thing he asked her to reassure him about; apparently everything else was quite settled in his mind, but he added that if she foresaw any difficulty in escaping he would find some way of facilitating her flight.

G. M. was sharper than his father. He meant to have his bird in hand before counting out his money. We discussed what line Manon was to take, and once again I did everything I could to get her to put the scheme out of her mind, pointing out all the risks; but nothing could shake her determination.

She wrote a short note to G. M., assuring him that she would have no trouble in going to Paris on the day in question and that he could confidently expect her. We then settled that I was to go at once and take new lodgings in some village on the far side of Paris, and move our few belongings with me. The following afternoon, that is to say on the day of her assignation, she should go in good time to Paris, and after receiving G. M.'s presents beg him to take her to the Comedy; she should take on her person as much of the money as she could carry and entrust the rest to my valet, whom she proposed to take with her. This was the same man who helped her to escape from the Hôpital, and he was devoted to us both. I was to have a cab ready at the corner of the Rue Saint-André-des-Arts, and at about seven o'clock leave it there and proceed under cover of darkness into the doorway of the theatre. Manon promised to make some excuse for leaving her box for a minute, and she would use that minute to come down and join me. The rest would be easy. In a trice we should get back to my cab and leave Paris by the Faubourg Saint-Antoine through which lay the road to our new home.

Far-fetched as it was, this plan sounded quite well concocted. But in reality it was absurdly rash of us to suppose that, even if it had gone off without a hitch, we could ever have evaded pursuit. And yet we laid ourselves open with the most foolhardy self-confidence. Manon left with Marcel, our valet. I felt very sad at seeing her go, and as I kissed her I said: 'You are not deceiving me, Manon? You will be true to me won't you?' She tenderly scolded me for my lack of trust, and repeated all her protestations.

Her idea was to get to Paris about three. I left a little later and went and froze all the afternoon at the Café de Féré, by the Pont Saint-Michel. I stayed there until nightfall and then left to take a cab which I posted at the corner of the Rue Saint-André-des-Arts, as we had arranged.[17] Then I walked to the door of the theatre. I was surprised not to find Marcel, who should have been waiting for me there. I waited patiently for an hour amidst a crowd of lackeys, anxiously scanning all the passers-by. At length, when it was well past seven and I had seen nothing with any bearing on our plan, I bought a ticket for the floor of the house in order to see whether Manon and G. M. were to be found in the boxes. They were not, either of them. I went back to the door, where I spent another quarter of an hour in a fever of impatience and anxiety. But I saw nothing, could not make up my mind to do anything definite, and so found my way back to the cab. The driver saw me and came forward a few steps to meet me, saying mysteriously that a pretty young lady had been waiting in the carriage for an hour. She had asked for me, giving a description that he recognized, and having been told that I was coming back she had said that she would not mind waiting. I supposed it must be Manon, and hurried on. But I saw a pretty little face that did not belong to her. It was a stranger, who began by asking if she had not the honour of addressing M. le Chevalier des Grieux. I said that was my name. She said she had a letter to give me that would explain why she had come and how she had the advantage of knowing my name. I asked her for time to read it in a nearby tavern. She insisted on coming too, advising me to ask for a private room. 'Who sent this letter?' I said as we went upstairs. She said I would find out when I read it.

I recognized Manon's hand. This is roughly what she said: G. M. had welcomed her with elegance and splendour beyond her wildest dreams. He had loaded her with gifts and held out before her the fortune of a queen. Notwithstanding, she did not forget me in her grand new surroundings, so she assured me, but as she had not been able to persuade G. M. to take her to the Comedy she had had to postpone the pleasure of seeing me until another day. But to make up a little for the disappointment she foresaw this news might give me, she had managed to procure me one of the prettiest girls in Paris, who was the bearer of her letter. Signed: Your faithful love, Manon Lescaut.

There was something to me so cruel and insulting in this letter, that for some time I remained suspended between rage and grief, and determined to make an effort to put the memory of my lying and thankless mistress out of my mind for ever. I glanced at the girl in front of me. She was exceedingly pretty, and I could have wished she were sufficiently so to make me forsworn and unfaithful in my turn. But I did not find those soft and lovely eyes, that godlike carriage, that complexion mixed in Love's own palette – in a word the inexhaustible wealth of charms which Nature had lavished on my faithless Manon. 'No, no,' I said, looking away from her, 'the perfidious creature who sent you knew quite well that she was giving you a fruitless errand. Go back to her, and tell her from me to enjoy her crime, and enjoy it without compunction if she can. I cast her off for ever, and all other women with her, for they could never be as charming as she is and are probably just as wicked and faithless.'

I was on the point of going downstairs and away, leaving behind me all claims on Manon, and, as the deadly jealousy rending my heart took the form of sullen and gloomy calm, I thought I was all the nearer being cured because I felt none of the violent reactions that had tortured me on similar occasions. But alas, I was just as much the dupe of love as I thought I was of G. M. and Manon.

The girl who had brought the letter, seeing me on the point of going downstairs, asked what message I wanted her to take back to M. de G. M. and the lady with him. The question made me turn back into the room, and with one of those sudden revulsions unbelievable to those who have never felt violent passion, I found myself thrown from the peace of mind I thought was mine into a terrible outburst of rage. 'Go and retail to the traitor G. M. and his wicked mistress the despair I have been plunged into by her accursed letter,' I said, 'but tell them they won't have the laugh of me for long, and that I shall strike them both down with my own dagger.' I dropped into a chair, and my hat fell to the floor on one side and my stick on the other, and tears began to run down my cheeks as my fit of rage turned into abject misery. I was reduced to weeping, groans and sighs. 'Come here, my child,' I said to the girl. 'Come here, since you have been sent to console me. Tell me whether you know of any consolation for rage and despair, any cure for a desire to make an end of oneself after killing two wretches who do not deserve to live.' She took a few hesitant steps towards me and I went on: 'Yes, come here, come and dry my tears and bring some peace back to my heart; say you love me, so that I can get used to being loved by someone else besides that deceitful woman. You are pretty; I might be able to return your love.' The poor child, who was not more than sixteen or seventeen, seemed to have more delicacy about her than most of her type, and she was extremely surprised by such strange behaviour, but still she came and tried to give me a few caresses. I immediately thrust her aside, however. 'What do you expect from me?' I said, 'you are a woman, you belong to a sex which I abominate and have finished with for good. The sweetness of your face is just another threat of treachery. Go away and leave me alone.' She curtseyed without daring to say a word, and made to go out. I called out to her to stop: 'But at least you might tell me why, how and for what purpose you were sent here. How did you know my name and find out where I was?'

She said that she had known M. de G. M. for some time, and that he had sent for her at five o'clock. She had gone with the lackey who had brought the message, and found herself in a grand house where he was playing piquet with a pretty lady. They had told her that she would find me in a carriage at the corner of the Rue Saint-André-des-Arts, and instructed her to give me the letter she had brought. I asked whether they had said anything else. She blushed, and said that they had given her to hope that I would take her to keep me company. 'Then they cheated you,' I said, 'they cheated you, poor girl. You are a woman, and what you need is a man. But he must be a rich and happy man, and you cannot find him here. Go back to M. de G. M., go back to him! He has everything necessary for winning the love of pretty women; he has furnished houses and carriages to give away. As for me, I have nothing to offer but love and constancy. Women scorn my poverty and use my simplicity for their sport.'

And I added a thousand pathetic or violent things according to which of my passions came uppermost. But at length through continual fretting I calmed down sufficiently to be able to reflect a little. I compared this last misfortune which those of the same kind I had already undergone, and I found that there was no more cause for despair in the one than in the others. I knew what Manon was: why go on upsetting myself about a misfortune I ought to have foreseen? Would it not be better to set about finding a remedy? There was still time. If I did not want to have to reproach myself for letting my troubles win by default, then at least I had better spare no pains in setting them right. Thereupon I began to consider all the means which might open a way to hope.

To attempt to snatch her from G. M.'s grasp by force was a

desperate method only likely to be my undoing and with no chance of being successful. But I felt that if I could have secured even a few words of private talk with her, I would undoubtedly have had some effect on her heart. I knew the vulnerable spots of that heart so well! I was so sure of being loved by her! I could have wagered that even this fantastic notion of sending a pretty girl to comfort me came from her and had its origin in her compassion for my sorrow. So I resolved to devote all my ingenuity to seeing her. Having turned several ways over in my mind, I finally settled on this one: the willingness with which M. de T. had begun to do me kindnesses was too clear for me to have any doubts left as to his sincerity and zeal. I decided to go to him at once and ask him to send for G. M., alleging urgent business. Half an hour was all I needed for seeing Manon. My plan was to find a way of getting into her room, and I thought that would be simple so long as G. M. were out of the way.

I felt easier in my mind when I had come to this decision. The girl was still there, and I paid her generously and took her address, giving her to hope that I would go and spend the night with her, which would prevent her wanting to return to those who had sent her. Then I went back to my cab and had myself driven as quickly as possible to M. de T.'s. On the way I was afraid I might not find him at home, but fortunately he was in, and in a very few words I told him my trouble and what I wanted him to do for me. He was so amazed to learn that G. M. had succeeded in seducing Manon that, all unaware of the part I myself had played in my own undoing, he generously offered to rally all his friends and get them to rescue my mistress by force of arms. I pointed out that a sensation of that kind might well be disastrous for Manon and me. 'No,' I said, 'let us save our blood for the last resort. I have in mind a more peaceful way which I hope will be no less successful.' He undertook unreservedly to do anything I asked, and when I repeated that all I wished him to do was to let G. M. know that he wanted to speak to him and then keep him out of the way for an hour or two, he set off with me at once to do his best for me.

We discussed what pretext he could use for delaying G. M. so
long. I advised him to begin by sending him a straightforward
note from some tavern, asking him to go there at once about a
matter so urgent that it would brook no delay. 'And then,' I
went on, 'I will watch out for his departure and get into the
house without any trouble, since the only people who know me
there are Manon and Marcel, who is my personal servant. Your
part of the business is this: by then you will have G. M. with
you, and you can tell him that the urgent matter you want to see
him about is one of money – you have just lost all yours at cards,
and pledged a great deal more with no better luck. He will need
some time to take you to his strong-box, and that will give me
enough to carry out my purpose.'

M. de T. followed out this arrangement to the letter. I left him
in a tavern where he at once wrote his note, took up my position
a few yards away from Manon's house, saw the messenger come
and G. M. leave immediately afterwards, followed by a lackey.
Angry though I was at her perfidy, I knocked at her door as
respectfully as at a temple. Luckily Marcel opened, and I signed
to him to hold his tongue. Although I had nothing to fear from
the other servants, I asked him in a whisper to take me to the
room where Manon was without my being seen. He said that
was quite easily done by going softly up the main staircase.
'Quickly, then,' I said, 'and try to prevent anybody else from
going up while I am there.' I reached her room without any
trouble.

Manon was reading. It was at that moment that I had cause to
marvel at that strange woman's character. Far from being afraid
or appearing embarrassed at seeing me there, she merely betrayed
the mild surprise which is involuntary when you see somebody
you think is far away. 'Ah, my dear, is it you?' she said, and came
and kissed me as tenderly as usual. 'Good Heavens! you are
daring! Who would have expected to see you today, and here,
too!' I did not return her caresses, but freed myself from her
arms, pushed her away with scorn and stepped back a pace or
two so as to keep her at a distance. This movement of mine did

not fail to disconcert her, and she remained fixed in the same position, turning pale as she looked at me. But in my heart I was so overjoyed at seeing her again that I could scarcely bring myself to say a hard word to her, despite all the grounds I had for being angry. Yet my heart was bleeding at the cruel outrage she had done me. I quickly called all this to mind in an attempt to fan the flames of my indignation, and I tried to make my eyes blaze with other fires than those of love. As I remained silent for some time and my agitation was apparent to her, she trembled, seemingly with fear.

I could not bear this. 'Oh Manon,' I said, and now my voice was full of tenderness, 'you false and perverse creature, how shall I begin to reproach you? I see you are pale and trembling, and I am still so affected by the slightest sign of sadness in you that I am all too anxious not to hurt you by my criticisms. Yet I do say this, Manon: the grief of your disloyalty has cut me to the heart. You cannot wound a lover like this unless you mean to kill him. This is the third time, Manon – oh yes, I have kept count – and such things cannot be forgotten. You must make up your mind what line you are going to take, and you must do so at once, for I am too sick at heart to stand up any longer to such brutal treatment. My heart is ready to break with grief, I feel it giving up the struggle. I cannot go on,' I finished, dropping into a chair, 'I can hardly find the strength to speak or stand up.'

She made no answer, but knelt down and put her head on my knees, with her face hidden in my hands which I at once felt wet with her tears. God! with what emotions I was torn at that moment! 'Oh, Manon, Manon,' I sighed, 'it is very late in the day to offer me your tears when you have led me to the brink of death. You are putting on a sadness you cannot be feeling, since I suppose your greatest worry at this moment is my presence here, for I have always stood in the way of your pleasures. Open your eyes. Look and see who I am; one does not shed tears for a poor devil one has heartlessly betrayed and thrown over.' She did not move, but fell to kissing my hands. 'You inconstant creature,' I went on, 'ungrateful and faithless woman, where are all your vows and promises? Most fickle and cruel of lovers, what have you done with that love you were swearing was mine even today? God of justice, is this the way a wanton laughs at You after having so piously called You to witness? Lying gets all the recompenses, then, whilst despair and loneliness are the rewards of constancy and fidelity!'

As I uttered these words there came to my mind such bitter thoughts that in spite of myself I began weeping. Manon realized this by the change in my voice, and at last she broke her silence: 'I suppose I must be very wicked,' she mused sadly, 'since I have given you such pain and grief, but may Heaven punish me if I thought I was, or even dreamed of becoming so.' These words struck me as so devoid of all meaning or good faith that I could not restrain a fit of violent anger. 'What disgusting play-acting!' I cried. 'Now I can see more clearly than ever that you are nothing but a liar and a whore. Now I know your mean little character. Good-bye, you despicable creature,' I said, rising to go, 'I would rather die a thousand deaths than have anything more to do with you. May Heaven punish me as well if I ever do you the honour of setting eyes on you again. Stay with your new lover, give yourself to him and hate me, give up honour and common sense; I can just laugh now, it's all the same to me!'

She was so frightened by this outburst that she remained on her knees by the chair which I had left, gazing at me, trembling and not daring to breathe. I moved on a few more steps towards the door, but with my head turned and my eyes fixed on her. But to harden my heart against such loveliness as hers I should have had to lose every human feeling, and I was so far removed from having such inhuman strength, that I suddenly flew from one extreme to the other, returned to her, or rather rushed without stopping to think, seized her in my arms and kissed her passionately. I implored her forgiveness for my fit of temper, admitted that I was a brute and unworthy of the happiness of being loved by a woman like her. I made her sit down and in my turn knelt before her and begged her to listen to me, there, as I was. On my knees I poured into my hurried apologies everything that an obedient and devoted lover can imagine to express his respect and adoration. I begged her, as an act of clemency, to say she forgave me. She dropped her arms round my neck and said that it was she who needed all my forbearance so that she could wipe away from my memory all the pain she had given me. She said that she was beginning to fear, and rightly, that I might not relish anything she had to say to justify herself. 'I!' was my immediate rejoinder; 'who am I to ask you for justifications? I approve of everything you have done. It is not for me to ask reasons for your behaviour. I am only too happy if you do not deny me your love, my dearest Manon. But,' I went on, as the thought of my present condition came back to me, 'how absolute your power must be, Manon, for you can make my joy and sorrow as you please. Now I have made humble amends and given proof of my repentance, may I speak of my sadness and sufferings? Am I to learn what is to become of me today, and whether you are going to sign my irrevocable death-warrant by spending the night with my rival?'

She took some time to think out her answer.

'My dear,' she said, and her tone was now quite calm, 'if you had explained all that at the outset, you would have spared yourself a great deal of sorrow and me a most distressing scene. Since your misery only comes from jealousy, I would have cured it by offering to follow you at once to the ends of the earth. But I imagined that it was the letter I wrote you under G. M.'s eyes and the girl we sent that had upset you. I thought you might have regarded my letter as a piece of mockery, and that girl (if you supposed she had come to you on my orders) as a declaration that I had given you up for G. M. It was this thought that threw me into a panic just now, for, all innocent as I was, it occurred to me when I came to think about it, that appearances were not very kind to me. However, I want you to be my judge when I have explained the true facts.'

She then told me everything that had happened since she found G. M. waiting for her where we now were. And certainly he had received her like the greatest princess in the world. He had shown her over all the rooms, which were in sumptuous and impeccable taste. Then he had counted out ten thousand livres in his study and had given them to her with some jewellery, including the pearl necklace and bracelets she had already had from his father. From there he had led her into a salon she had not yet seen in which she had found an exquisite meal served. She was waited on by new servants he had engaged for her with instructions to treat her as their mistress. Finally he had taken her to see the coach, horses and all the other presents, after which he had suggested a game of cards to while away the time until supper. 'I admit,' she said, 'that I was impressed by all this magnificence, and it seemed to me that it would be a pity to spoil our chances of so much money in the long run, by merely being content to disappear there and then with the ten thousand francs and the jewels. Here was a fortune ready to drop into our hands, and you and I might live very comfortably at G. M.'s expense. Instead of suggesting the theatre, I took it into my head to sound him about you, so as to get an idea of our chances of seeing one another if my plan came off successfully. I found him very easy to manage. He asked me what I felt about you and whether I had any regrets about leaving you. I said that you were so charming and had always been so good to me that it was hardly to be expected that I could dislike you. He admitted that you were a good fellow and that he had been drawn to you as a friend. He wanted to know how I thought you would take my leaving you, particularly when you found out that I was in his hands. I told him that our love affair was already of such long standing that our passion had had time to cool off somewhat; also that you were rather uneasy about it, and might not take losing me as a very great disaster, because it would free you from a burden which you were beginning to find irksome. I added that I had not found it difficult to allege that I was going to Paris on business, because I knew that you would not make a fuss, and that you had agreed and come along yourself and not seemed particularly upset when I had left you. "If I thought," he said, "that he would be prepared to be on good terms with me, I

would be the first to pay my respects and offer him my services."
I said that from what I knew of your character I was sure that
you would respond to such a gesture, especially if he could
render you some assistance in your business affairs, which had
been in a precarious state since you had broken with your family.
He hastened to say that he would do you any service that lay in
his power, and even, supposing you felt inclined to embark on
another love affair, procure you a pretty girl he had just given up
in order to live with me. I applauded this idea as to forestall any
suspicions he might have, and, becoming more and more en-
amoured of my scheme, I only wished I could find a way of
letting you know what was afoot, for fear of your being too
alarmed when you missed me at the meeting-place. That is why I
suggested his sending you this new mistress that very evening; it
was so as to have a pretext for writing to you. I was obliged to
have recourse to this trick because I could not expect him to
leave me free for a single moment. My proposal made him laugh.
He called for his lackey, asked him if he could find his ex-mistress
at once, and dispatched him here and there in search of her. He
thought that she would have to go to Chaillot to find you, but I
told him that when I left you I had promised to meet you at the
theatre or, if anything prevented my going there, you had undertaken to wait for me in a carriage at the corner of the Rue
Saint-André. Therefore, I thought, we had better send your new
young lady there, if only to save you from freezing at the street
corner all night. I also said that it would be advisable to write
you a line to explain the exchange, which otherwise you might
find a little difficult to understand. He agreed, but I had to write
in his presence, and I was careful not to put things too explicitly
in my letter. And that,' Manon concluded, 'is how things
happened. I am keeping nothing back, either of what I did or of
what I proposed to do. The girl came, she struck me as pretty
and, as I felt sure that my absence would make you unhappy, I
was quite sincere in wishing that she might alleviate a little of
your boredom, for the fidelity I expect of you is that of the heart.
I would have been only too glad to send you Marcel, but I could

not find a single moment to tell him what I wanted you to know.' At length she wound up her story by recounting how vexed G. M. had been when he received M. de T.'s letter. 'He hesitated,' she said, 'as to whether he should leave me, and promised to be back without delay. That is why I cannot see you here now without uneasiness, and why I looked so surprised when you came.'

I HEARD this tale through very patiently. It is true that it contained many cruel and mortifying things from my point of view, for her disloyal intentions were so clear that she had not even taken the trouble to disguise them. She could hardly expect G. M. to leave her alone all that night like a vestal virgin, and it was therefore with him that she proposed to spend it. What an admission to make to a lover! And yet I reflected that I was partly responsible for her doing this, through having made G. M.'s sentiments known to her in the first instance and through my complaisance in blindly lending myself to the rash idea of this adventure. Besides, by a natural reaction peculiar to my type of mind, I was impressed by the candour of her story and by the frank and open way she retailed even circumstances most calculated to give me offence. I told myself that there was no malice in her sins; she was fickle and imprudent but straightforward and honest. Moreover, of course, love was in itself enough to shut my eyes to all her misdeeds. I was only too delighted at the prospect of snatching her back from my rival that very night. And yet I said to her: 'And with whom would you have spent tonight?' The question, and the misery in my voice as I put it, threw her off her guard, and she only answered in disjointed *buts* and *ifs*. I took pity on her embarrassment, changed the subject and said flatly that I expected her to follow me there and then. 'Yes, I would like to,' she said, 'but don't you approve of my plan, then?' 'Oh, isn't it enough,' I answered, 'that I approve of everything you have done up to now?' 'What,' she replied, 'aren't we even to take away the ten thousand francs? He has given them to me. They are mine.' I advised her to leave everything behind and only think about getting away promptly, for although

I had been with her for less than half an hour, I was afraid that
G. M. might come back. However, she was so pressing in her
entreaties to make me agree not to go away empty-handed that I
felt I had to concede something after obtaining so much from
her.

While we were getting ready to go I heard a knock at the
street door. I was sure it must be G. M., and in the flurry I was
thrown into by this thought I cried out to Manon that if he came
in he was a dead man. And it was quite true that I had not
sufficiently recovered from my recent emotions to be able to see
him and keep my self-control. But Marcel put an end to my
anxiety by coming in with a note for me which had been handed
in at the door. It was from M. de T., and informed me that
G. M. had gone off to his house to find some money, and so he
had taken advantage of his absence to pass on a most amusing
idea of his; it seemed to him that the most enjoyable way I could
take revenge on my rival would be to eat his supper and spend
the night in the bed he was hoping to share with my mistress.
This seemed quite simple to do, he thought, if I could find three
or four men bold enough to hold him up in the street and
trustworthy enough to keep him under their eyes until the next
day. For his part, M. de T. undertook to keep him amused for at
least another hour with various matters he had ready for his
return. I showed this note to Manon and explained to her the
trick I had used in order to gain free admission into her house.
She was vastly amused by my ingenuity and M. de T.'s, and we
gave ourselves up to a few minutes of uncontrolled merriment.
But when I treated this latest idea as a joke, to my surprise she
seriously urged me to do it, saying that the scheme delighted her.
In vain did I ask where she expected I could find, all of a sudden,
men who could waylay G. M. and hold him in safe custody. She
said that I might at least try, since M. de T. guaranteed us
another hour, and when I raised further objections she accused
me of being tyrannical and having no consideration for her. She
thought it was the prettiest plan in the world: 'You will have his
place at supper, sleep between his sheets and early tomorrow

carry off his mistress and his money. You will be well revenged on both father and son.'

Despite the secret promptings of my heart, which seemed to forbode some dreadful disaster, I gave in to her entreaties. I went out, intending to get two or three guardsmen I had known through Lescaut to take on the job of waylaying G. M. I only found one at home, but he was an enterprising fellow, and no sooner had I told him what was afoot than he promised me it should come off. He asked only for ten pistoles to share out among three guardsmen whom he proposed to employ under him. I begged him to waste no time. I waited at his house while he rounded them up, which he did in less than a quarter of an hour, and when he was back with his accomplices, I myself took him to the corner of a street through which G. M. must necessarily pass on his way back to Manon's. I told him not to handle G. M. roughly, but to keep him under close watch until seven in the morning, so that I could be sure he would not escape. He said that he planned to take him to his own room, make him undress and even lie on his bed, while he and his three stalwarts spent the night playing cards and drinking. I stayed with them until G. M. came into sight, and then I withdrew a few paces into a dark corner to witness this extraordinary scene. The guardsman accosted him, pistol in hand, and explained civilly that it was not his money or his life he was after, but that, if he made the least trouble about following him or uttered the slightest sound, he would blow his brains out. G. M., seeing him backed by three soldiers, and probably fearing he might receive the full charge from the pistol, offered no resistance. I saw him led away like a sheep. Then I went straight back to Manon, and, to allay any suspicions the servants might have, I mentioned as I came in that there was no point in waiting supper for M. de G. M., because he was detained by business that could not be neglected and had asked me to come and apologize for him and dine with her; which, I said, I regarded as a great honour with so charming a lady. She played up well to this stratagem, and we sat down to the meal, keeping a very dignified air so long as the lackeys were there serving us. When we had finally dismissed them, we had one of the most delightful evenings of our lives. I secretly ordered Marcel to find a cab and have it ready at the door before six in the morning. At about midnight I pretended to take my leave of Manon, but slipped back again quietly with Marcel's help, and made ready to occupy G. M.'s bed, just as I had taken his place at table. At that very moment our evil genius was working for our undoing. While we were given up to the raptures of love, the sword was suspended above our heads by a single thread which was about to snap. But so that you can fully appreciate all the circumstances of our ruin I must elucidate its cause.

When G. M. was held up by the guardsman he had a lackey following him. This fellow, terrified at the mishap that had befallen his master, ran back the way he had come, and the first move he made to help him was to go and inform old G. M. of what had occurred. Naturally he was most alarmed at such disquieting news. He was extremely active for his age, and this was his only son. First he questioned the lackey about everything his son had done that afternoon – had he quarrelled with anybody, or taken part in somebody else's quarrel? Had he been in any questionable house? The lackey, believing his master to be in deadly peril, thought that now he ought not to hold anything back that might help to save him, and divulged all he knew about his affair with Manon, the money he had laid out on her, how he had spent the afternoon in the house until about nine o'clock, how he had then gone out, and the trouble he had got into on his return. It was enough to make the old man suspect that the root of the business must be some quarrel over a woman. By then it was at least half past ten, but he did not hesitate to go at once to the police and have special orders issued to all the squads of the watch. He obtained a squad to go with him, and in all haste made for the street where his son had been stopped; then he visited every place in the town where there might be some hope of finding him, but, picking up no trace of him, he finished by having himself taken to the woman's house, where he thought his son might have returned.

Old G. M.

He arrived just as I was getting into bed. Our door was shut and I did not hear the knock at the street door. However, he gained admission, together with two officers, inquired in vain what had happened to his son and took it into his head to see his son's mistress, in case she might be able to throw some light on the affair. He climbed the stairs, with the two men still at his heels. We were just going to get into bed when he opened the door. The sight of him froze my blood. 'Oh God!' I said to Manon, 'it's old G. M.!' I leaped for my sword, but, as ill-luck would have it, it was entangled with my belt. The officers saw my move and at once came up and wrenched it away from me. They quickly had me defenceless. A man is helpless in his shirt.

Flustered as he was, G. M. did not take long to recognize me, and it was still easier for him to recall Manon. 'Is this an illusion?' he said pompously. 'Do I not see the Chevalier des Grieux and Manon Lescaut?' I was beside myself with shame and vexation, and made no answer. For a short time he seemed to be turning various thoughts over in his mind, and as though they had suddenly kindled his anger he turned to me and shouted: 'You wretch! You have killed my son. I am sure you have.' Stung by this insult, I proudly retorted: 'You old villain, if I had had to kill any of your family I should have begun with you.' 'Hold on to him!' he said to the archers. 'He has got to give me news of my son. Unless he tells me at once what he has done with him, I shall have him hanged tomorrow.' 'You'll have me hanged, will you?' I shouted back. 'You swine, it is people like you who ought to be seen on the gallows. You had better know that my blood is nobler and purer than yours. Yes, I know what has happened to your son, and if you annoy me any more I'll have him strangled before tomorrow dawns, and I promise you the same fate after him.'

It was rash of me to admit I knew where his son was, but I was so furious that I let this indiscretion escape me. He at once called five or six other officers who were waiting outside the door, and ordered them to make sure of all the servants in the house. 'Ha! Monsieur le Chevalier,' he went on in sarcastic tones, 'you know where my son is and you will have him strangled, will you? Well, you can rest assured that we shall see to that.' I immediately realized the blunder I had committed. He went up to Manon, who was sitting weeping on the bed, and treated her to a few sardonic gallantries about the sway she held over father and son and the good use she was making of it. The abominable old lecher then made as if to take a few liberties with her. 'Keep your hands off her!' I cried, 'or else there would be nothing sacred enough in the world to stop me laying hands on you.' He went out, leaving in the room three of the men whom he ordered to see that we put on our things at once.

I do not know what his plans for us were at that stage. If we had told him where his son was we might have gained our freedom. As I was putting on my clothes I wondered whether that was not the wisest policy. But if such was his intention when he left our room he had changed his mind when he returned. He had been and questioned Manon's servants, whom the officers had arrested. He could not find out anything from the servants his son had engaged for her, but when he knew that Marcel had previously been in our employ, he determined to use intimidation to make him speak.

Marcel was a loyal fellow, but simple and ignorant. The memory of what he had done to free Manon from the Hôpital, together with the terror inspired by G. M., made such an impression on his feeble wits that he imagined he was going to be taken straight to the gallows or the wheel, and promised to reveal everything that had come to his knowledge if only his life were spared. This satisfied G. M. that there was something more serious and criminal in our affairs than he had hitherto supposed, and he offered Marcel not only his life but also a reward for a confession. The poor devil told him the part of our plan which we had not hesitated to discuss in front of him because he was to have had some share in it. It is true that he was quite unaware of the modifications we had made in Paris, but when we left Chaillot he had been told the outline of the scheme and the part he was to play in it. So he told G. M. that our object was to swindle his son and that Manon was to receive, or had already received, ten thousand francs which, we intended, should never revert to the heirs of the house of G. M.

Having found out all this, the old man rushed up to our room in a towering rage, and without a word went through to the inner sanctum, where he had no difficulty in finding the money and the jewels. He came back to us purple in the face and, holding out in front of us what he chose to call our plunder, poured out violent insults. He dangled the pearl necklace and bracelets close to Manon's face. 'Do you recognize them?' he jeered. 'It was not the first time you had seen them. The very same ones, well I never! They appealed to your taste, my dear, I can see that. Poor children,' he added, 'they are really quite nice, both of them, but a bit on the tricky side.'

My heart was bursting with rage at these insulting remarks. For a single minute's freedom I would have given ... Good God, what wouldn't I have given! However, by dint of a great effort I said with a moderation which was only a refinement of anger: 'Let us call a halt to these insolent witticisms, Sir. What is it all about? What do you propose to do with us?' 'This is what it is all about, Monsieur le Chevalier,' he answered, 'it is a question of going straight to the Châtelet. Tomorrow we shall have some daylight and we shall see more clearly into the matter, and I hope that in the end you will do me the kindness of telling me where my son is.'

I did not need to reflect very long in order to understand that once shut up in the Châtelet we should be exposed to terrible consequences. I trembled as I foresaw all the dangers. Notwithstanding all my pride, I realized that I must give way to the force of my destiny and flatter my cruellest enemy in the hope of getting something out of him by submissiveness. In courteous tones I asked him to listen for a moment. 'I see my faults in their true light, Sir,' I said, 'and admit that my youth has led me to commit grave offences, and that you have grounds for complaint after having been so wronged. But if you know the power of love, if you can conceive what a poor young man must be suffering when all he has in the world is being taken away from him, you will perhaps think I might be forgiven for having tried to enjoy some slight revenge, or at least that I have been punished enough by the humiliation I have just been through. There is no need for prison or torture to discover your son's whereabouts. He is in safe hands. I had no intention of hurting him or offending you. If you will do me the favour of setting us free, I am prepared to name the place where he is spending a peaceful night.' Far from being touched by my entreaties, the old brute laughed and turned his back on me. He merely let fall a few words to the effect that he knew all about our scheme. As for his son, he callously added that as I had not killed him he would turn up safe and sound. 'Take them off to the Petit Châtelet,' he said to the officers, 'and mind the Chevalier does not give you the slip. He is a wily bird and has already got out of Saint-Lazare.'

He went out, and you can imagine the state he left me in. 'Oh Heaven!' I cried, 'I am ready to bear patiently all the blows that come from you, but that a miserable wretch like that should have the power to tyrannize over me in this way is enough to bring me to the depths of despair.' The soldiers asked us not to keep them waiting any longer: they had a carriage at the door. I gave Manon my hand to lead her downstairs. 'Come, my beloved queen,' I said, 'come and face all the bitterness of our destiny. Some day it may please Heaven to make us happier.'

[handwritten annotation:] out of keeping noble + elevated

WE WENT off in the same coach. She fell into my arms. I had not heard her say a word since G. M.'s arrival, but when she found herself alone with me she poured forth a thousand endearments and bitterly reproached herself for being the cause of my misfortune. I assured her that I would never complain of my fate so long as she continued to love me. 'I am not the one to be pitied,' I said, 'a few months of prison have no terrors for me, and anyhow I shall prefer the Châtelet to Saint-Lazare. But my heart bleeds for you, my dearest. What a fate for so charming a creature! How can Heaven deal so harshly with the most perfect of its works? Why were we not born with qualities more in keeping with our miserable lot? We have been given intelligence, taste and feeling, but oh, what a sorry use we are making of them! To think that so many base souls, just made for our fate, enjoy all the favours of fortune!' Such thoughts as these filled my heart with grief. But that was nothing beside my forebodings for the future, whilst fear for Manon withered my very soul. She had already been an inmate of the Hôpital, and, even if she had left that institution by the front door, I knew that further offences of the same kind would entail extremely dangerous consequences. I would have liked to confide my fears to her, but was frightened of passing on too much of them to her. I trembled for her but dared not warn her of her peril, and I held her in my arms and sighed so as to convince her at least of my love, for love was almost the only sentiment I dared express. 'Manon,' I said, 'tell me truly, will you always love me?' She answered that it made her very unhappy to think that I could call that into question. 'Very well,' I said, 'I do not, and with that knowledge I am ready to defy all our enemies. I will use my

121

family influence to get out of the Châtelet, and if I do not get you out as soon as I am free myself, then all my blood will be worth nothing.'

We reached the prison and were separated. I was prepared for this, and so it was less hard to bear. I recommended Manon to the concierge, letting him know that I was a man of some position, and promising him a considerable reward. I kissed my beloved mistress before parting from her, urged her not to be too downcast and to fear nothing so long as I was alive. I was not without money, and I gave her some and out of the remainder I paid the concierge for a month's full board in advance, for herself and for me.

My money had a very good effect, for I was put into a decently furnished room and was told that Manon had a similar one. I at once set about finding ways and means of getting free. Clearly there was nothing absolutely criminal in my case, and even assuming that our intention to commit a theft was proved by Marcel's deposition, I knew perfectly well that mere intentions are not punishable. I determined to write at once to my father and ask him to come to Paris himself. As I have already said, I was less ashamed of being in the Châtelet than at Saint-Lazare. Also, although I still had all due respect for paternal authority, my timidity had been considerably lessened by age and experience. So I wrote; and the people at the Châtelet raised no objection to allowing the letter to go. But I might have spared myself the trouble if I had known that my father was to reach Paris on the next day.

He had had the letter written by me eight days previously,[18] and it had given him great joy. But, however rosy the hopes I had held out of my conversion, he had not thought fit to rely altogether on my promises. He had made up his mind to come and witness my change of heart with his own eyes, and to let his next move be guided by the sincerity of my repentance. He arrived the day after my imprisonment. First he called on Tiberge, to whom I had to ask him to send his reply, but he could not find out from him either where I was or what I was doing at the moment. All he could gather from him were the main things that had happened to me since my escape from Saint-Sulpice. Tiberge gave him a very reassuring account of my leanings towards virtue as expressed in our last talk, adding that he thought I had broken altogether with Manon, but he was surprised that I had not given him any news of myself for a week. My father was not taken in. He sensed that there was something behind the silence Tiberge complained of that had escaped his penetration, and he took such pains to follow up my tracks that two days after his arrival he found out that I was in the Châtelet.

Before his visit, which I was far from expecting so soon, I had one from the Lieutenant-General of Police, or rather, to call things by their proper names, I underwent an interrogation. He criticized my conduct, but not harshly or unkindly, gently pointing out that my way of life filled him with pity and that I had been unwise to make an enemy of such a man as G. M. True, he said, it was easy to see that my troubles were due to frivolity and imprudence rather than to malice aforethought, but the fact remained that this was the second time I found myself under his jurisdiction, and he had hoped that I would have learned more wisdom after the two or three months of lessons I had had at Saint-Lazare. I was delighted to have such a reasonable judge to deal with, and answered his questions so respectfully and with such moderation that he seemed most satisfied with my replies. He urged me not to give myself up too much to despondency, and said that he felt disposed to do what he could for me out of consideration for my family and extreme youth. I ventured to put in a word for Manon and to extol her gentleness and good character. He laughingly replied that he had not yet seen her, but that she was said to be a dangerous woman. This so moved my loving heart that I defended my poor mistress in an impassioned speech, and indeed could not refrain from shedding tears. He ordered me to be taken back to my room. As I went out, this dignified magistrate exclaimed: 'Oh, love, love, will you never be reconciled with wisdom?'

I was sadly turning over my thoughts and going over the conversation I had had with the Lieutenant-General, when I heard my door open: it was my father. I ought to have been half prepared to see him, since I expected him a few days later, but all the same I was so overcome that I would have leaped into the depths of the earth if it had opened at my feet. I went forward and embraced him with extreme embarrassment. He sat down. Neither of us had yet said a word.

I remained standing there with head uncovered and downcast eyes. 'Sit down, Sir,' he said severely, 'sit down. Thanks to the scandal caused by your debaucheries and fraudulent practices, I have discovered where you are. The advantage of your sort of merit is that it cannot remain hidden. You are on the infallible road to fame. I look forward to all this ending at the Grève, and hope you will have the real glory of being displayed there for everybody's admiration.'

I made no answer. He went on: 'How a father is to be pitied when, having tenderly loved his son and spared no pains to make a good man of him, all he finds in the end is a rogue who dishonours him! You can get over a reverse of fortune: time softens the blow and your bitterness fades away. But what remedy is there for an evil which grows day by day, such as the excess of a vicious son who has lost all sense of honour? You have nothing to say, you villain?' he added. 'Look at the modesty he is putting on, and that hypocritical air of gentleness! Wouldn't you take him for the most perfect gentleman ever born?'

Although I had to admit that I deserved some of these insults, yet it seemed to me that he was going too far. I thought the time had come for me to explain my point of view simply and naturally. 'I assure you, Sir,' I said, 'that the humility you see in me as I stand before you is in no way put on; it is the natural attitude of a true-born son who has infinite respect for his father, especially when that father is displeased. Nor do I claim to pass for the most virtuous man of our race. I know I deserve your strictures, but I implore you to season them with a little more kindness, and not to treat me like the lowest of criminals. I do not merit such hard names. You know that the cause of all my misdeeds is love. What a fatal passion it is! Do you know its power; can it be that your blood, which is the source of mine, has never burned with the same fires? Love has made me too soft, too passionate, too faithful and perhaps over-indulgent of the desires of a most charming woman; and that is the sum of my crimes. Do any of these things dishonour you, do you think? Please, father,' I added affectionately, 'have a little pity for a son who has always been devoted to you and full of respect, who has not turned his back on honour and duty as you think, and who is a thousand times more to be pitied than you can imagine.' By the time I finished these words I was in tears.

A father's heart is Nature's masterpiece. She reigns therein, so to speak, with indulgence, and controls its every movement. My father, who in addition to being a father was a man of intelligence and taste, was so touched by the form in which I had cast my apologies that he could not conceal his change of heart. 'Come along, my poor boy,' he said, 'come here and kiss me. You make me sorry for you.' I did so. I could tell what he was feeling by the way he held me to him. 'But how are we to set about getting you out of here?' he said. 'Tell me the whole story and don't hold anything back.' As there was nothing in my behaviour, taken all round, which was completely dishonourable – at least when it was compared to that of young men of a certain set – and as a mistress is not considered anything to be ashamed of nowadays, any more than a little manipulation in winning at cards, I described the life I had been leading in a detailed and candid manner. But with each misdeed I acknowledged, I was careful to complete an illustrious parallel, so as to mitigate the shame of it. 'I am living with a mistress,' I said, 'without being bound by the ties of marriage. The Duke of ***** flaunts two in the eyes of all Paris; M. de ***** has had one for ten years and he has loved her with a devotion he never had for his wife. Two thirds of the most respected men in France are proud to do the same. I have gone in for a certain amount of trickery at the gaming-table: the Marquis of ***** and the Count of ***** have no other source of income, and the Prince of ***** and the Duke of ***** are leaders of a band of knights of the same order.'[19] As for my designs on the two G. M.s' money, I could have proved just as easily that my conduct was not unexampled, but I still had too much sense of honour left to accuse myself together with all the people I could have cited as precedents; and so I merely begged my father to forgive this lapse and ascribe it to the two violent passions which had dominated me: revenge and love. He asked whether I could give him a few suggestions as to the quickest methods of gaining my liberty in a way which would avoid publicity. I told him how kindly disposed the Lieutenant-General of Police was, and said that if he met any difficulty it could come only from the G.M.s; it would therefore be to the point if he took the trouble to go and see them. He promised to do so. I dared not ask him to intercede for Manon. This was not for want of courage, but rather because of my fear of scandalizing him by such a proposal and of putting into his head some idea which might be fatal to her and me. To this day I ask myself whether this fear of mine was not the cause of my greatest misfortune, in that it prevented my testing my father's feelings and trying to bring him to think more favourably of my unhappy mistress. I might once again have aroused his compassion, and I would certainly have put him on his guard against the impressions he was going to be too ready to receive from old G. M. Who can tell? Even then my evil destiny would perhaps have triumphed over all my efforts; but at least I might only have had my destiny and the cruelty of my enemies to blame for my undoing.

After leaving me, my father went and called on M. de G. M. He found him with his son, whom the guardsman had duly set free. I have never heard the details of their conversation, but it is all too easy to guess what they were by the terrible results. Together they went – the two fathers, I mean – to the Lieutenant-General of Police, and asked two favours of him: one, to let me out of the Châtelet immediately, and the other, to keep Manon shut up for the rest of her days or to send her to America. At that time they were beginning to transport a number of undesirable characters to the Mississippi. The Lieutenant-General of Police gave them his word to ship Manon off on the first boat. M. de G. M. and my father came at once and brought me the news of my reprieve. M. de G. M. spoke very civilly about the past, congratulated me on having such a good father and exhorted me to benefit henceforward by his precepts and example. My father ordered me to apologize for the supposed wrong I had done to G. M.'s family and thank him for having joined with him to secure my freedom.

We all left together without a word having been said about my mistress. I did not even dare to mention her name to the warders in their presence. But my poor recommendations would have been quite useless, for the cruel order had gone through at the same time as the one setting me free. An hour later the unhappy woman was taken to the Hôpital and put with some outcasts of society condemned to the same fate. My father made me go with him to the house where he was staying, and it was nearly six in the evening before I found a chance to slip away and return to the Châtelet. All I hoped to do was to have some comforts sent to Manon and to urge the concierge to look after her well, for I did not suppose that I should be granted permission to see her. And I had not yet had time to think over ways of setting her free.

I asked for the concierge. My kindness and liberality had pleased him and he felt disposed to do his best for me, so he referred to Manon's fate as a calamity bitterly to be deplored because it must hurt me so. I did not understand what he was talking about, and for a moment or two we were at cross purposes. Seeing at length that some explanation was called for, he gave me the one I have already had the horrible experience of telling you, and which I must now go through again. No apoplectic stroke ever had a more sudden and devastating effect. The beating of my heart was so painful that as I fell unconscious to the floor, I thought I was being delivered from this life for ever. And even when I came to, something of this thought remained in my mind, for I let my gaze roam all round the room and back to myself in order to find out whether I still was that most unhappy thing, a living man. Certain it is that had I followed the natural human tendency to look for a way out of trouble, nothing could have seemed more welcome than death in that moment of despair and consternation. Religion itself could offer my imagination nothing more unbearable in the after-life than the cruel torments which racked me. Yet, such is love's power to work miracles, I soon found enough strength to thank Heaven for having restored my consciousness and reason; for my death would have been useful only to me, while Manon needed my life to save her, help her and avenge her. I vowed to spare myself nothing to that end.

The concierge gave me all the help I could have expected from the best of friends, and I accepted his services with the keenest gratitude. 'So you are touched by my sufferings!' I said. 'Everybody has forsaken me. Even my father, it seems, is one of my most implacable persecutors. Nobody has any pity on me. You alone, in this abode of cruelty and savagery, show compassion for the most unhappy of men!' He advised me not to show myself in the street until I had somewhat recovered from the distressed state I was in. 'Oh, never mind that,' I said as I left him, 'I shall be seeing you again sooner than you think. Get ready the blackest of your dungeons, for I am going to do my best to deserve it.'

And, indeed, my first impulse was nothing less than to get rid of the two G. M.s and the Lieutenant-General of Police, and then swoop down on the Hôpital at the head of an armed band consisting of everybody I could enlist in my quarrel. Even my father would scarcely have been spared in what seemed my just revenge, for the concierge had not concealed from me that he and G. M. were the authors of my ruin. But when I had walked a few steps down the street and the air had cooled down my blood and temper a little, my rage gradually gave way to a more reasonable frame of mind. The death of our enemies would have been of very little use to Manon, and it might have led to my being deprived of every way of helping her. Besides, would I ever have resorted to a cowardly murder? What other way could I find for revenge? I concentrated all my strength and all my mind on the first task, which was to set Manon free, and I put off everything else until after that vital undertaking had met with success. I had little money left. But money was the indispensable starting-point. I could think of only three people from whom I could expect to get any: M. de T., my father and Tiberge. There seemed little likelihood of getting anything from the last two, and I was ashamed of wearying the other with my importunities. But in desperate straits there is no room for delicacy, and I made straight for the seminary of Saint-Sulpice, without caring whether I was recognized or not, and asked for Tiberge. His first words showed me that as yet he knew nothing about my latest escapades, and that made me change my intention of working on his pity. So I talked in general terms about how happy I was to have seen my father again, and then asked him to lend me some money on the pretext that, before leaving Paris, I had a few debts to settle that I wished to keep unknown. He at once offered me his purse. I took five hundred francs out of the six hundred I found there, and offered him my note of hand, but he was too generous to accept it.

From there I went on to M. de T. I kept nothing from him, but told him the whole tale of my woes and misfortunes. He already knew it down to the minutest detail, because he had taken the trouble to follow the fortunes of young G. M., but he heard me out and expressed deep sympathy. When I asked his advice about how to liberate Manon, he gloomily answered that he could see so little chance of it that we must give up all hope, short of a miracle from Heaven. He had purposely called at the Hôpital himself, since she had been sent there, but had not been able to get permission to see her; the Lieutenant-General of Police had issued the strictest orders. As the crowning disaster, the party of unfortunates which she had to join was to set off two days from then. His news so numbed me with horror that he might have gone on talking for an hour and I should never have thought of interrupting him. Then he explained that he had not come to see me at the Châtelet, because it would be easier for him to help me if they thought he had no connexion with me. During the few hours since I had left there, his ignorance of my whereabouts had made him very uneasy, for he had wanted to see me at once so as to give me the only advice capable of leading to any change in Manon's fate; but it was a dangerous piece of advice, and he begged me never to divulge that he had any responsibility for it. It was to choose a few stalwarts brave enough to attack Manon's escort after it had left Paris. He gave me no time to mention lack of money, but presented me with a purse and said: 'Here are a hundred pistoles which may be of some use to you. You can return them when fortune has put your position to rights again.' He added that if his own reputation had allowed him to take a hand personally in rescuing Manon, he would have put his arm and sword at my disposal.

His wonderful kindness brought the tears to my eyes, and I showed my gratitude with all the enthusiasm I could summon up in my distress. I asked him whether there was anything to be hoped for from direct intercession with the Lieutenant-General. He said he had already thought of that, but had decided that method was useless, because there was no point in appealing for a reprieve of this nature without just grounds, and he could not see what reason could be invoked for interceding with so highly placed and influential a person. If any hopes of success by such means could be entertained, they could only come by softening the hearts of M. de G. M. and my father and inducing them to beg the Lieutenant-General to revoke his sentence. He offered to do everything in his power to win over young G. M., although he thought his friendship for him had cooled off somewhat, owing to suspicions he had entertained about his having a hand in our affair. Finally he urged me, for my part, not to neglect any means of bending my father's will.

This was no easy undertaking for me; there was not only the natural difficulty I should find in overcoming his determination, but also another reason which made me afraid even to meet him: I had run away from his lodgings in defiance of his orders, and was determined not to go back now I had found out the cruel fate reserved for Manon. I rightly feared that he would have me forcibly detained and taken away into the country. My elder brother had used that method once before. It is true that I was older now, but age was a feeble argument against force. However, I thought of a way which would save me from that danger: it was to have him summoned to a public place and get myself announced under another name. I decided to adopt these tactics. M. de T. went off to G. M.'s house and I went to the Luxembourg, whence I sent word to my father that a gentleman was waiting to pay him his respects. I feared he might have some trouble in coming, as it was nearly nightfall; but in a short time he appeared, followed by a lackey. I invited him to walk down an avenue where we could be undisturbed. We walked on for at least a hundred yards in silence. No doubt he thought that so many precautions had not been taken without some important reason, and he waited for my speech while I thought out how I was going to put it.

At last I began: 'Sir,' I said in a trembling voice, 'you are a good father and you have shown me infinite kindness and forgiven numberless misdeeds. And Heaven is witness that I have all the sentiments of a loving and dutiful son. But it seems to me . . . that your severity . . .' 'Well, what about my severity?' father broke in, no doubt finding my slowness trying to his patience. 'Oh, Sir,' I went on, 'I feel that you are being unnecessarily severe in the treatment you have meted out to poor Manon. You have sought advice from M. de G. M., and in his hatred he has painted her in the blackest colours. You have formed a dreadful picture of her, and yet she really is the sweetest and most lovable creature that ever lived. Why has not Heaven inspired you to want to see her just for a moment? I am no more certain that she is charming than that you would have found her so. You would have taken her part. You would have come to loathe the shady intrigues of G. M. and would have taken pity on her and me. Yes, I know you would. Your heart is not made of stone, and it would have been softened.' Seeing me holding forth with an enthusiasm that would not have let me stop talking for some time, he cut me short again, wanting to know what I proposed to achieve by such an impassioned speech. 'I am begging you for my life,' I answered, 'for I cannot hold on to it for a moment once Manon has gone to America.' 'No, no,' he said sternly, 'I would rather see you without life than without virtue and honour.' 'Then let us not go a step further,' I cried, seizing him by the arm; 'take this hateful and unbearable life away from me, for in the despair into which you have cast me, death will be a boon. It is a fitting gift from a father's hand.'

'I should only be giving you what you deserve,' he retorted; 'I know many a father who would not have waited as long as this to be your executioner, but my over-fondness has been your ruin.'

I threw myself at his feet. 'Oh! if you have any affection left,' I said, clasping his knees, 'do not harden your heart against my tears. Remember I am your son. Think of my mother. You loved her so dearly! Would you have let her be snatched from your arms? No, you would have defended her with your life. Have not others a heart just like yours? Can anybody be so heartless when once he has known what love and suffering are?'

'Don't say another word about your mother,' he angrily replied; 'the very thought makes me boil with indignation. If she had lived to see your debaucheries, they would have killed her with grief. That is enough of this talk. It is only making me angry and it will certainly not make me change my decision. I am going home, and I order you to follow me.' The hard and sharp tone in which he issued this command made it abundantly clear that he was inflexible. I moved a few steps off, fearing that he might take it into his head to stop me with his own hands. 'Do not add to my desperation,' I said, 'by forcing me to disobey you. I cannot follow you; it is impossible. It is equally impossible for me to live after the harsh way you have treated me. So it is good-bye for ever. You will soon hear of my death, and perhaps that will revive your paternal feelings.' I turned to go away. 'So you refuse to follow me?' he cried in a rage. 'Then be off with you and go to perdition. Good-bye, thankless and rebellious son!' 'Good-bye, cruel and unnatural father!' I shouted back in a transport of fury, and strode out of the Luxembourg.

I RUSHED through the street like one possessed, until I came to M. de T.'s house. As I went along, I raised my eyes and hands and called upon the heavenly powers. 'Oh, God,' I said, 'will You be as pitiless as mankind? I have no other help now but You.'

M. de T. had not yet come back, but he arrived after I had been waiting a few minutes. He was crestfallen, for his mission had succeeded no better than mine. Young G. M. was less incensed against Manon and me than his father was, but he was not willing to make any representations on our behalf. He had excused himself on the grounds of his own fear of that vindictive old man, who had already treated him to a scene and upbraided him for his intended intimacy with Manon. So the only way left open to me was brute force along the lines sketched out by M. de T., and I concentrated all my hopes on that. 'Such hopes are very precarious,' I conceded, 'but the best-founded one, and the most comforting to me, is that at least I may perish in the attempt.' I asked him to help me with his good wishes, and took my leave of him. From then onwards my only concern was to collect some comrades in whom I might kindle some spark of my own courage and determination.

The first person to come to my mind was the guardsman whom I had employed to hold up G. M. Moreover, I hoped to spend the night in his room, as I had had too much on my mind during the afternoon to think about finding lodgings. I found him alone. He was delighted to see me safely out of the Châtelet, and offered me his help in the most friendly way. I explained what I wanted him to do for me. He was shrewd enough to realize all the difficulties, but generous enough to try to surmount them. We discussed my plan well into the night. He referred to the three soldiers he had used on the last occasion as good fellows who could be relied upon in a tight corner. M. de T. had told me exactly how many guards were to escort Manon: there were to be only six. Five bold and determined men were enough to scare off such miserable hirelings, who are not capable of defending themselves honourably when the dangers of a fight can be avoided by cowardice. I was not without money, and the guardsman advised me not to be niggardly if I wanted to be sure that the attack came off successfully. 'We need horses,' he said, 'with pistols and a musket for each man. I will undertake to see to these preparations tomorrow. We must also have three civilian suits for the soldiers, who would never dare to be seen in uniform in an affair of this kind.' I gave him the hundred pistoles I had had from M. de T., and they were spent the next day to the last sou. I reviewed my three soldiers, heartened them with big promises and, to allay any misgivings, started by making each one a present of ten pistoles. When the appointed day came, I sent one of them early in the morning to the Hôpital to spy out the hour at which the soldiers were to set out with their victims. Although I took this precaution only out of excessive anxiety and foresight, it turned out to be absolutely necessary. I had relied on false information about the route they were to take, and, feeling sure that this pitiful band was to be put on ship at La Rochelle, I should have wasted all my efforts and waited on the Orleans road. But thanks to my soldier's report, I now knew that they were taking the Normandy road and that the departure for America was to take place from Havre.

We made straight for the Porte Saint-Honoré, taking care to go through different streets, and we met again on the outskirts of the city. Our horses were fresh, and we soon spied the six guards and the two wretched wagons you saw two years ago at Pacy. The sight all but deprived me of strength and consciousness. 'Oh, Fortune,' I cried, 'cruel Fortune! at least vouchsafe me in this hour death or victory!'

We held a brief council of war on the method of our attack.

The guards were not more than four hundred paces ahead, and we could intercept them by crossing a little field round which the highroad took a bend. My guardsman advised taking that route so as to surprise them by a sudden charge. I agreed, and was the first to spur on my horse. But inexorable Fortune had turned a deaf ear to my prayer.

The guards, seeing five horsemen bearing down upon them, realized that they were being attacked and took up the defensive positions, fixing their bayonets and levelling their guns with a resolute air. This only served to put fresh courage into the guardsman and me, but it took all the spirit out of our three craven companions. They stopped dead as if by an agreed signal, exchanged a few words I could not hear, turned their horses and galloped away towards Paris.

'My God!' said the guardsman, as panic-stricken as I was by such an infamous desertion, 'what are we to do now? There are only two of us.' I was speechless with rage and astonishment, and pulled up, uncertain whether my first revenge ought to be to pursue the wretches who had left me in the lurch. I watched them galloping out of sight and then glanced at the guards. Had I been able to cut myself in two, I would have charged simultaneously on these two objects of my rage and destroyed them together. The guardsman could tell the dilemma I was in by the shifting of my eyes, and he urged me to listen to him: 'There are only two of us,' he said, 'and it would be madness to attack six men as well armed as we are ourselves and apparently determined to make a stand. We must go back to Paris and try to be more lucky in our choice of men. That escort cannot cover much ground in one day with those two cumbersome wagons, and we shall easily catch them up again tomorrow.'

I considered this course of action for a moment, but, seeing nothing on all sides but reasons for despair, I came to a truly despairing decision. It was to dismiss my companion with thanks for his help and then, far from attacking the guards, go up to them and humbly ask them to let me join their band, so as to accompany Manon to Havre and then sail overseas with her. I turned to the guardsman. 'Everybody persecutes or betrays me,' I said, 'and I have no more faith left in anybody. I have nothing more to hope for from destiny or human aid. My cup of misfortune is full; all I can do is accept it and shut my eyes to all hope. May Heaven reward your kindness! Farewell! I am going to help my cruel fate to accomplish my ruin by deliberately meeting it half way.' He tried to make me return to Paris, but in vain. I begged him to leave me at once and let me follow out my resolve, lest the guards might think we still meant to attack them.

I slowly went towards them alone, and my face was so woebegone that they could not have found anything alarming about my approach. All the same, they stood at the ready. 'Gentlemen,' I said as I came up to them, 'rest assured, I do not bring war, but come to ask favours.' I asked them to go on their way without suspicion, and as we went along I told them the favours I wanted. They consulted together as to how they would receive such an overture. The head of the band, speaking for the rest, answered that their orders were to keep their prisoners under the closest watch, but that, as I seemed a nice fellow, he and his friends would relax their discipline a little. But I must understand that they could not do it for nothing. I had about fifteen pistoles left, and frankly told them what my reasons were. 'Very well,' he said, 'we will treat you generously. It will only cost you one écu per hour to see whichever of our young ladies you like best. That is the usual Paris rate.' I had not made any special reference to Manon, because I did not intend them to know about my passion. At first they imagined that it was just a young man's whim that made me want to get a bit of amusement with these creatures, but when they thought they saw that I was in love, they put up their prices so much that my purse was empty by the time we left Mantes, where we had spent the night before we reached Pacy.

Can I tell you of the heartrending talks with Manon during that journey, or the impression I had when the soldiers gave me leave to go up to her cart? Words never can convey more than half the feelings of the heart: but try to picture my poor Manon chained by the waist, sitting on a few handfuls of straw, with her weary head resting against the side of the cart. Her eyes were continually shut, but her pallid face was wet with a trickle of tears flowing from beneath her lids. She had been too listless to open them, even when she had heard the noise made by the guards when they were afraid of being attacked. Her clothes were dirty and disordered and her delicate hands exposed to wind and weather. That enchanting frame, that face capable of taking the whole world back to the days of idolatry, was reduced to an indescribable state of slovenliness and neglect. For some time I rode by the side of the cart and gazed at her. I had so little control of my emotions that more than once I nearly had a bad fall. My frequent sighs and exclamations made her open her eyes and glance at me. She recognized me, and I noticed that her first impulse was to leap out of the wagon and come to me, but her chain held her down and she relapsed into her original attitude. I asked the guards to stop a moment out of pity, and they did so out of greed. I left my horse and sat beside her. She was so exhausted and dejected that a long time passed before she could utter a sound or move her hands. I moistened them with my tears. I could not find a single word to say, either, and we both remained in the most pitiful state that has ever been known. Even when we had recovered our power of speech, our words were no less miserable. Manon said little: it seemed as though shame and grief had affected her very organs of speech, for her voice was weak and tremulous. She thanked me for not having forgotten her and, she added with a sigh, for giving her the satisfaction of seeing me once again to say a last farewell. When I assured her that nothing could tear me away from her, that I was minded to follow her to the ends of the earth to care for her, serve her, cherish her and bind my wretched fate to hers for ever, the poor girl gave way to such an outburst of love and sorrow that I feared such violent emotion might endanger her life. Every feeling in her soul seemed concentrated in her eyes, which she kept fixed on me. Now and again she opened her mouth, but had not the strength to finish the few phrases she began. But a few sentences did escape her: words of wonder at my love, tender concern at the excess of it, doubt that she could really be so happy as to have inspired such perfect devotion, pleading to make me give up this idea of following her and seek some other happiness more worthy of me, which, she said, I could not hope to find with her.

In spite of the unsurpassable harshness of my destiny, I found my happiness in her eyes and in the knowledge that she loved me. True, I had lost all that other men value, but I was master of Manon's heart, and that was the only wealth I cared for. What did it matter to me where I lived, in Europe, in America? Little did I care if I could be sure of the bliss of living with her. Is not the whole universe the dwelling-place of two faithful lovers? Do they not find in each other father, mother, family, friends, wealth and felicity? If anything gave me cause for anxiety, it was the fear of seeing Manon exposed to poverty and want. Already I pictured myself with her in some wilderness inhabited by savages. But I told myself that there could never be savages as cruel as G. M. and my father, for at least they would let us live in peace. If accounts were to be believed, they lived according to the laws of nature, knowing neither the mad lust for money that possessed G. M., nor the fantastic notions of honour which had turned my father into my enemy. They would not interfere with two lovers when they saw them leading as simple a life as theirs. Thus I was reassured in that direction, but I harboured no romantic illusions about the ordinary needs of daily life. Too often already I had experienced that there are some privations not to be borne, especially by a delicately reared girl accustomed to a life of ease and plenty. I was exasperated that I had emptied my purse so uselessly and that the little money I had left was on the point of being filched by these rascally soldiers. It seemed to me that, with a modest sum, I might have hoped not merely to keep poverty at bay for some time in America, where money was scarce, but even to come to some arrangement whereby I could have a settled livelihood. This train of thought led me to the idea of writing to

Tiberge, whom I had always found so ready with offers of friendship and help. I wrote from the next town we passed through; but though I admitted I was bound for Havre, where I was taking Manon, I did not volunteer anything else beyond the pressing need of money I knew I should be in when I arrived there. I asked him for a hundred pistoles, payable by the post-master, and said that he would realize that this was the last time I should prey upon his friendship, for my unhappy mistress was being taken from me for ever, and I could not let her go without a few comforts that might alleviate her sufferings and my own mortal grief.

When the soldiers discovered how passionately I was in love, they became so unreasonable that they constantly put up the price of their slightest favours, and soon had me reduced to the utmost poverty. In any case I was too much in love to think of money. From morning till night I stayed by Manon's side, lost to the world, and time was no longer measured out to me by the hour but by whole days. Eventually, when my purse was quite empty, I found myself exposed to the whims and bullying of six brutes, who treated me with insufferable condescension. You saw that for yourself at Pacy. My meeting you there was a blessed moment of relief which fortune granted me. The compassion which the sight of my woes inspired in you was the only recommendation I had to your generous heart, and the help you so freely gave me enabled me to reach Havre. The soldiers kept their promise more faithfully than I had hoped.

We arrived at Havre. First I went to the post. Tiberge had not had time to reply. I asked exactly when I could expect his letter. It could not be there for two or more days and, by a strange caprice of my cruel fate, it turned out that our ship was to sail on the morning of the day when the post arrived. My despair cannot be described. 'What!' I exclaimed, 'even in misfortune must I always be singled out for extremes?' 'Alas,' Manon replied, 'is such an unhappy life worth the trouble we are taking over it? Let us die at Havre, my beloved, let death put a speedy end to our sufferings. Shall we go and drag out our lives in some unknown land where we must certainly expect horrible privations since I am being sent there for a punishment? Let us die,' she repeated, 'or at least, you put an end to my life and go and seek a happier lot in the arms of some more fortunate woman.' 'No, no,' I said, 'for me it is an enviable lot to be unhappy with you.' Her words made me shudder, for it seemed to me that her misfortunes had got the better of her. I therefore tried to assume a calmer manner in order to divert her mind from death and despair. I resolved to keep up the same attitude in the future, and since then I have found nothing succeeds more in putting new heart into a woman than a courageous air in the man she loves. When I had lost hope of help from Tiberge I sold my horse, and the money I got for it, together with what remained of your kind gift, made up the small sum of seventeen pistoles. Seven of these I spent on a few necessary comforts for Manon, and carefully put aside the other ten for a nucleus of our hopes and fortune in America. I had no trouble about being taken on the ship, for young men ready to join the colony were then in demand, and my food and passage were given me free of charge. The Paris mail was due out on the next day, and I left a letter for Tiberge. It was a pathetic letter and evidently capable of stirring him deeply, since it made him take a decision which could come only from infinite love and generosity for a friend in need.

We set sail. The weather continued favourable. The captain allowed Manon and me a place apart, and was good enough to look upon us with a kindlier eye than he had for the rest of our miserable associates. On the very first day I had a private talk with him and, in order to secure a little personal consideration, told him part of the tale of my misfortunes. I did not think I was guilty of a shameful lie in telling him that I was married to Manon. He pretended to believe it and took me under his protection. We had proofs of this throughout the crossing. He went out of his way to see that we were properly fed, and his many little attentions earned us the respect of our companions in misery. I was continually concerned to see that Manon did not suffer the slightest discomfort. She appreciated what I did, and this knowledge, together with a keen sense of the strange pass to which I had let myself be brought for her sake, made her so tender and devoted, so anxious on her side to minister to my smallest needs, that we were continually vying with each other in love and services. I did not hanker after Europe, but, on the contrary, the nearer we came to America the more I felt my heart open out into tranquillity. If I could have been sure that when we got there we should not lack the bare necessities of life, I would have thanked destiny for having granted so favourable a turn to our woes.

AFTER a voyage lasting two months, we at length touched the shore we so longed to see. The first glimpse of the country was anything but pleasant. Nothing but bare and uninhabited earth, with here and there some reeds and a few trees blasted by the wind. Not a sign of man or beast. However, when the captain had fired a few volleys, we soon saw a group of citizens of New Orleans making for us with demonstrations of great joy. So far we had not seen the town, which is hidden from that side by a little hill. They welcomed us as if we had dropped from Heaven. These poor folk eagerly plied us with questions about the state of France and the various provinces where they had been born, and embraced us like beloved friends and brothers who had come to share their poverty and loneliness. With them we set out for the town; but, as we came nearer, we discovered with surprise that what up to then we had heard praised as a fine city was merely a collection of miserable hovels, inhabited by five or six hundred souls.[20] The governor's house seemed to stand out a little in height and situation. It is defended by a few earthworks, surrounded by a broad moat.

First we were introduced to him. He had a long colloquy with the captain, and then came over to us and examined one by one the women who had come on the ship. There were thirty of them, for at Havre we had been joined by another party. After a long scrutiny, the governor sent for various young men of the town who had been pining for wives. He awarded the prettiest to the more senior ones, and the rest were distributed by lot. So far he had not spoken to Manon, but when he had ordered the others away he made us both stay behind. 'The captain tells me you are married,' he said, 'and that during the voyage he has recognized your intelligence and character. I will not go into the reasons which have brought about your misfortune, but if it is true that you are as well bred as your appearance suggests, I will spare no pains to make your life as pleasant as possible, and you on your side will help me to find some enjoyment in this wild and desolate place.' I answered in the way I thought most likely to confirm the good opinion he had of us. He gave orders for a lodging to be made ready for us in the town and kept us to supper. He struck me as very civilized for the head of a colony of wretched outcasts. He did not ask us any questions in public about the details of our story, but the conversation remained general, and, despite our depression, Manon and I did our best to make it agreeable.

In the evening he had us taken to the house made ready for us. It was a humble shack made of planks and mud, with two or three rooms on the ground floor and a loft above. The governor had had five or six chairs put in, and a few other articles necessary for daily life. The sight of this sorry dwelling made Manon look horrified, but she was much more upset on my behalf than on her own. When we were left alone, she dropped into a chair and began sobbing bitterly. At first I tried to console her, but when I realized that her concern was for me alone and that in our common sufferings she was thinking only of what I had to bear, I put on a bold front and even simulated gaiety so as to communicate some to her. 'What have I to complain of?' I said. 'I have everything I desire. You love me, don't you? And what other joy have I wished for? Let us leave our fate in God's hands; it does not look as desperate as all that to me. The governor is a civilized person; he has shown some consideration for us and will not let us go without necessities. As for the poverty of our hut and the primitive furniture, you may have noticed that few people here seem better housed and furnished than we are. And besides,' I added with a kiss, 'you are a wonderful alchemist: you change everything into gold.'

'Then you will be the richest person in the universe,' she answered, 'for if there has never been a love like yours, it is equally impossible to be loved more tenderly than you are. I know what I am,' she went on, 'and I know full well that I have never been worthy of the wonderful affection you have for me. I have hurt you in ways you could never have forgiven but for your unfailing goodness. I have been frivolous and fickle, and even while loving you passionately, as I have always done, I have never been anything but graceless. But you cannot imagine how I have changed. The tears you have seen me shed so often since we left France have never once been for my own troubles, for I ceased to feel them as soon as you began to share them with me. No, I have only wept out of love and pity for you. I cannot console myself for having given you a single moment's pain in my life. Over and over again I blame myself for my inconstancy, and my heart aches when I think what love has made you capable of doing for an unhappy woman all unworthy of it, and who,' she ended with a flood of tears, 'if she gave all the blood in her body, could never repay half the sorrow she has brought upon you.'

Her tears, her words and the tone in which they were uttered made such a profound impression upon me that my very soul seemed to split asunder. 'Be careful, dearest Manon,' I said, 'be careful. I am not strong enough to bear such tokens of your love; I am not used to such excesses of joy. Oh, God!' I cried, 'I have nothing more to ask. I am assured of Manon's heart, and that heart disposed as I have always wished it to be for my happiness; I shall never again cease to be happy. My felicity is established for ever.' 'Yes it is,' she answered, 'if you let it depend on me, and I know full well where I can rely on finding mine.' These delightful thoughts transformed my hut into a place fit for the greatest king in the world, and I lay down to sleep. Thereafter America seemed an enchanted land. 'New Orleans is the place to come to,' I often said to Manon, 'if you want to taste the true sweetness of love. Here love is free from self-interest, from jealousy and inconstancy. Our fellow-countrymen come here in search of gold; little do they imagine that we have found far more priceless treasures.'

We were careful to cultivate the governor's friendship. A few weeks after our arrival, he was good enough to give me a small post which happened to fall vacant at the citadel. It was not a very distinguished position, but I accepted it as a boon from Heaven, for it enabled me to live without depending on anybody else. I took a man for myself and a maid for Manon. Our little fortune settled into a routine. My life was exemplary and so was Manon's, and we neglected no opportunity of making ourselves useful or of doing good to our neighbours. Our sociable disposition and the gentleness of our manners earned us the confidence and affection of the whole community. In a short while we were so well thought of that we ranked as the leading people in the town after the governor.

The innocence of our pursuits and the unbroken peacefulness of our lives gradually brought our minds back to thoughts of religion. Manon had never been an unbeliever, nor was I one of those extreme freethinkers who glory in adding irreligion to depraved living. All our follies had been due to love and immaturity. Now experience was beginning to take the place of age, and it had the same effect upon us as ripeness of years. Our conversation was always serious, and imperceptibly it led us to a desire for virtuous love. I was the first to suggest the change to Manon. I knew her real principles. She was direct and natural in all her feelings, a quality which always inclines one towards virtue. I pointed out that our happiness lacked one thing only: the blessing of Heaven. 'We are both too sound in heart and soul,' I said, 'to go on living in defiance of our duty. It is true that we did so in France, where it was equally impossible for us to give up loving each other and to satisfy our love in a lawful way; but here in America, with nobody to depend on but ourselves and no further obligation to observe the arbitrary laws of social standing and public opinion, where indeed we are thought to be married, what is there to prevent our being so in fact, and purifying our love by the vows authorized by the Church? For my part, I am not offering you anything new when I give you my heart and hand, but I am prepared to renew that gift at the altar.' I could see that these words filled her with joy. 'Do you know,' she said, 'I have thought about this a thousand times since we have been in America? I have kept the wish locked up in my heart for fear of displeasing you, for I do not presume to aspire to the position of being your wife.' 'Ah, Manon,' I replied, 'you would soon be the wife of a king, if Heaven had brought me into the world with a crown. We must not hesitate any more. We have no obstacle to fear. I mean to speak to the governor about it this very day, and confess that up to now we have deceived him. Leave it to commonplace lovers to fear the indissoluble ties of marriage. They would not be afraid of them if they were as sure as we are of always being bound by those of love.' Having come to this decision I left Manon in an ecstasy of joy.

I am convinced that there is not a decent man living who would not have approved of my views in the circumstances in which I found myself, that is to say enslaved by a fatal passion I could not overcome, and assailed by remorse I would never be able to stifle. But will anybody be found to accuse me of complaining unjustifiably, if I bewail God's cruelty in frustrating a design I had formed only to please Him? Frustrating, do I say? He punished it as though it were a crime. He had patiently borne with me so long as I walked blindly along the paths of sin, and His harshest chastisements were held in store for when I began to return to virtue. I fear I shall never have the strength to finish the story of the most tragic event that ever befell.

As I had agreed with Manon, I went to see the governor to ask his consent to the ceremony of our marriage. I would not have mentioned the matter to him or anybody else, if I could have been sure that his almoner, who was the only priest in the town, would have done me this service without his knowledge; but, not daring to hope that the almoner would promise to keep it a secret, I had elected to act openly.

The governor had a nephew, named Synnelet, of whom he was very fond. He was a man of thirty, brave, but hot-tempered and passionate. He was unmarried. From the very day of our arrival Manon's beauty had made an impression on him, and the numberless occasions he had had of seeing her for nine or ten months had so inflamed his passion that he was secretly pining away for her. But as he, like his uncle and everybody else in the town, was convinced that I was really married, he had conquered his love to the extent of keeping it unobserved, and had even shown his friendship for me by offering me his services on more than one occasion. When I reached the citadel I found him with his uncle. I saw no reason for keeping my intentions secret from him and made no difficulty about going into the matter in his presence. The governor heard me with his usual kindness. I told him part of our story, which he gladly listened to, and when I asked him to be present at the ceremony I had in mind he generously undertook to bear all the expense of the celebrations. I came away very pleased.

An hour later I saw the almoner come into our house. I imagined he was coming to give me a few instructions about the wedding; but he greeted me coldly and then stated in a word or two that the governor ordered me to put it out of my mind. He had other plans for Manon. 'Other plans for Manon!' I exclaimed, horror-struck. 'What plans, pray, Monsieur l'Aumônier?' He answered that I was not unaware that the governor was the master; Manon had been sent from France for the colony, and he had the right to dispose of her. He had not done so until then because he thought that she was married, but, having learned from me that she was not, he thought fit to give her to M. Synnelet, who was in love with her. My temper got the better of my prudence. I haughtily ordered the priest out of my house, vowing that the governor, Synnelet and the whole town put together should never dare to lay a hand on my wife, or mistress, as they chose to call her.

I at once told Manon the awful message I had received. We concluded that Synnelet had talked his uncle round since I had left, and that this was the culmination of some long-thought-out plan. They had force on their side. Here we were in New Orleans, as though in the middle of the sea: that is to say, cut off by measureless spaces from the rest of the world. Where could we run away? To some unknown country, either a wilderness or peopled by savage beasts and men equally savage? I was well thought of in the town, but I could not hope to win people's hearts sufficiently to make them give me help proportionate to my need. For that I should have wanted money, and I was poor. Anyhow, there was no relying on popular feeling, and if luck abandoned us our disaster would be irremediable. I turned all these thoughts over in my mind and discussed some of them with Manon. I thought of new ideas without waiting for her comments. As fast as I made one decision, I gave it up for another. I talked to myself and answered my own questions aloud – indeed my agony of mind cannot be compared with anything, because there has never been anything comparable. Manon's eyes were fixed on me and my emotion told her how grave the danger was. Trembling for me more than for herself, in her tender solicitude the poor girl dared not even open her mouth to put her fears into words.

After thinking things over and over, I came to the decision to go and see the governor, and try to influence him by considerations of honour and by reminding him of my past respect for him and his affection for me. Manon wanted to prevent my going. With tears in her eyes she said: 'You are going to your death. They will kill you. I shall never see you again. I want to die before you.' I had to make a great effort to persuade her that I must go and that she must stay at home. I promised that I would be back in an instant. Little did she know, or I either, that it was on her, and not on me, that all the wrath of Heaven and the fury of our enemies was to fall.

I went to the citadel and found the governor with his almoner. In an attempt to touch his heart, I stooped to grovelling humility that would have made me die of shame had I had recourse to it for any other reason. I worked on him with every method that could melt any heart save that of a wild and ferocious tiger, but the monster had only two answers to all my appeals, and he repeated them a hundred times: Manon was at his disposal and he had given his word to his nephew. I had steeled myself to keep the utmost self-control, and I merely said that I thought he was too good a friend to wish for my death, which I would certainly face rather than lose my mistress.

When I left him I was only too sure that nothing was to be hoped for from this obstinate old man, who would have seen himself damned a thousand times for his nephew's sake. But I kept to my resolution to preserve the outward signs of moderation to the very end. I was resolved, however, in the event of flagrant injustice, to give America one of the most horrible and bloody spectacles love has ever produced. On my way home, as I was thinking this project over, fate, bent on hastening my destruction, made my path cross that of Synnelet. He read some of my thoughts in my eyes. I have already said he was brave. He came boldly up to me and said: 'Aren't you looking for me? I know my intentions offend you and I realized that it would have to come to a fight between us. Let us go and see which of us is to be the lucky one.' I answered that he was right and that only my death could put an end to my claim. We went a hundred paces or so out of the town and crossed swords. I wounded and disarmed him almost at the same moment. He was so incensed by this mishap that he refused to sue for his life or give up his claim to Manon. Perhaps I had the right to deprive him of both there and then, but birth and breeding will out. I threw him back his sword. 'Let us start again,' I said, 'and remember, no quarter!' He came at me with indescribable fury. I must admit that I was no great swordsman, not having had more than three months instruction in Paris, but love guided my blade. Synnelet succeeded in running his sword through my arm, but I caught him on the return and dealt him such a powerful blow that he fell motionless at my feet.

In spite of the joy of victory after a mortal combat, I immediately realized what the consequences of the death of this man would be. I could not expect any pardon or delay of execution. Knowing as I did the governor's passion for his nephew, I was certain that my death would not be deferred a single moment after his was known. Immediate though this peril was, it was not the main cause of my panic. Manon, her interests, the danger she was in and the certainty of losing her, so confused me that my vision was obscured and I did not recognize the place where I was standing. I envied Synnelet's fate, for my own speedy end seemed the only way out of my terrible situation. But it was this very thought which promptly brought me back to my senses, and made me capable of coming to some decision. 'What!' I said to myself. 'Am I thinking of dying to end my own troubles? But can there be any such that I am more afraid of than losing the woman I love? No, I must face even the most dire extremities to help her, and until all those sufferings have been in vain, I must put off all thought of death.' I turned back towards the town and went home. Manon was half dead with terror and anxiety. She revived on seeing me again. I could not hide from her the terrible thing that had just happened. When I told her of Synnelet's death and my wound, she fell lifeless in my arms. It took me over a quarter of an hour to bring her back to consciousness.

I was only half alive myself. I could not see the slightest chance of safety for her or me. 'Manon, what are we to do?' I said, when she was a little more herself again. 'What are we to do? I must go away from here. Do you want to stay in the town? Yes, you stay here. You may still find happiness, and I shall go far away and seek death at the hands of savages or from the claws of wild beasts.' Weak as she was, she stood up, took my hand and led me to the door. 'We must leave together,' she said, 'there is not a minute to lose. Suppose they have found Synnelet's body. We might not have time to get away.' I felt distracted. 'But, my dear Manon,' I said, 'tell me where we can go. Can you see any way out? Would it not be better for you to try to live here without me and let me give myself up to the governor?' But this suggestion made her only all the more anxious to be going. I had to follow her. But before doing so I had enough presence of mind to go and get some spirits I had in my room, and fill my pockets with food. Our servants, who were in the adjoining room, were told that we were going for an evening walk, which we used to do every day. We hastened out of the town more quickly than would have seemed possible in Manon's delicate state.

I was still uncertain where we could find refuge, but I was not without hope of two possibilities; had it not been so I would have preferred death to the anxiety of not knowing what might happen to Manon. During the ten months of our stay in America I had learned enough about the country to know how the natives could be dealt with. It was quite possible to give oneself up to them and yet not go to a certain death. I had even learned a few words of their language and something of their customs on the various occasions I had had of seeing them. In addition to this slender resource there was another: the English, who, like us, have trading stations in this part of the New World.[21] But the distances were frightening; in order to reach their colonies we had to traverse great stretches of desert several days' journey in extent, and cross mountains so high and steep that they were difficult to negotiate even for the toughest and hardiest of men. Nevertheless I clung to the hope that we might make use of these two resources: the savages might help us to reach our objective and the English might welcome us into their homes.

We walked on as long as Manon's courage kept her going, that is to say about two leagues, for her matchless devotion made her refuse to stop sooner. At last, overcome by weariness, she had to admit that she could not go on any further. Night had already fallen. We sat down in the middle of a great plain, not having been able to find a single tree to shelter us. Her first care was to change the bandages she had tied on my wound before we set out. It was useless for me to try to stop her, and it would have put the finishing touch to her troubles if I had refused her the satisfaction of seeing me comfortable and out of danger before thinking about her own welfare. For some time I let her have her way, but I did so in silence and felt ashamed. But when she had satisfied all the promptings of her love, how eagerly I let mine have their turn! I stripped off my clothes and laid them beneath her so that she might feel the ground less hard. Despite her protests, I made her let me do everything I could think of to lessen her discomfort. I warmed her hands with my burning kisses and the heat of my breath, and spent the whole night watching over her and praying Heaven to grant her soothing and peaceful sleep. Oh God, how sincere and heartfelt were my prayers, and by what harsh decree did You decide not to lend an ear to them!

Forgive me if I finish the story in a few words, for it is killing me to tell it. I am relating a tragedy without parallel, and I am destined to bewail it for the rest of my days. But although these events are ever present in my memory, my soul seems to recoil in horror every time I attempt to put them into words.

We had spent part of the night quietly enough. I thought my beloved was asleep and scarcely dared to breathe for fear of disturbing her. At dawn I touched her hands and noticed that they were cold and trembling. I held them to my breast to warm them. She felt the movement, made an effort to grasp my hands and murmured faintly that she thought her last hour had come. At first I took these words for the sort of language ordinarily used in misfortune, and I merely answered with tender and consoling words of love. But her frequent gasps for breath, her failure to answer my questions, the pressure of her hands as she continued to cling to mine, told me that the end of her trials was near. Do not ask me to describe what I felt, or to report her last words. All I can find to say about that dreadful hour is that I lost her, and that I received tokens of her love even as she was passing.

My soul did not follow hers. Perhaps God did not think my chastisement hard enough, for He has ordained that I must drag on my life in weariness and misery. I have no wish to be any happier ever again.

There I stayed for more than twenty-four hours with my lips pressed to my beloved Manon's face and hands. And there I meant to die, but at the beginning of the second day the thought came to me that after my death her body would be exposed to ravening beasts. So I resolved to bury her and then await death on her grave. I was so weak through grief and lack of food that I was already near the end, and had to make repeated efforts to hold myself up. I had to resort to the spirits I had brought with me, and they gave me strength for the melancholy rites I had to perform. As the place was a sandy plain, I had no difficulty in making a hole. I broke my sword so as to use it for digging, but it was not as useful as my hands. I opened a wide trench and into it I committed the idol of my heart, having first wrapped her in all my clothes lest the sand should touch her. But first I kissed her a thousand times with all the tenderness of perfect love. I could not bring myself to close her grave, but still sat for a long time contemplating her. But at length my strength began to ebb again, and, fearing to lose it altogether before my task was done, I laid for ever in the bosom of the Earth the most perfect and lovely thing she ever bore. Then I lay down on the grave, turned my face to the sand, closed my eyes intending never to open them again, asked God to help me, and eagerly waited for death. You will find it hard to believe that, all through my mournful task, no tear fell from my eyes nor did any sigh escape my lips. My profound dejection and firm resolve to die had checked all the normal expressions of grief and despair. Nor did I stay long in that position before losing what little feeling and awareness I had left.

After what you have heard, the conclusion of my story is of so little consequence that it does not merit the trouble you are so kindly taking to listen to it. Synnelet's body was carried back into the town, and when his wounds were examined, it was found not only that he was not dead but that he had not even been seriously hurt. He told his uncle what had passed between us, and his generosity made him lose no time in spreading abroad the story of mine. I was sent for, and my absence together with Manon's gave rise to suspicions that we had fled. It was too late to track me down, but the next day and the day after were spent in searching for me. They found me on Manon's grave and seemingly dead, and those who found me in that condition, almost naked and bleeding from my wound, did not doubt that I had been robbed and murdered. They carried me back to the town, and the motion revived my senses. The sighs and groans that escaped me as I opened my eyes and found myself among the living told them that I was still in a state to receive succour. It was given, all too successfully. All the same, I was confined in a secure prison, and the case against me was drawn up. As Manon had disappeared, I was charged with having done away with her in a fit of jealous rage. I told them the pitiful story without any affectation. Despite the sorrow my tale renewed in him, Synnelet was generous enough to plead for my pardon, which was granted. I was so weak that I had to be carried from my prison to my bed, where I remained seriously ill for three months. My hatred of life did not lessen. I ceaselessly called upon death, and for a long time obstinately refused all remedies. But, having punished me so severely, God saw fit to make my sufferings and His chastisements useful to me. He shed His light upon me and brought back thoughts worthy of my birth and upbringing.[22] Some peace began to return to my soul, and this change was closely followed by my bodily recovery. I occupied myself wholly with honourable thoughts and meanwhile fulfilled the tasks of my little situation, while awaiting the vessels from France which call in this part of America once a year. I had made up my mind to return to my country and to atone for the scandal of my conduct by a good and regular life. Synnelet had had my dear mistress's body removed to an honourable place.

One day, about six weeks after my recovery, I was walking alone by the shore when I saw a trading ship arriving at New Orleans. I watched the people disembark, and to my extreme surprise I recognized Tiberge amongst those making their way towards the town. My faithful friend recognized me from far off, in spite of the changes sorrow had wrought in my face. He told me that the sole purpose of his voyage had been his anxiety to see me and to urge me to return to France. Having received the letter I wrote him from Havre, he had made his way there to give me personally the help I had asked for, and had been very distressed to find that I had sailed. Had there been a ship about to leave, he would have set off at once after me, but he had spent several months looking for one in various ports. At length, at Saint-Malo, he had found a ship about to weigh anchor for Martinique, and he had embarked in the hope of being able to find a passage easily from there to New Orleans. On the way the Saint-Malo ship had been captured by Spanish corsairs and taken to one of their islands. He had escaped from there by a ruse, and after various travels here and there, had managed to find a small ship which happily had just arrived and brought him back to me.

I could not express enough gratitude to a friend of such untiring devotion. I took him home and made him free of all I possessed. I told him everything that had happened to me since leaving France, and gave him unexpected joy by declaring that the seeds of virtue he had sown long ago in my heart were beginning to bear fruit which he would approve of. He assured me that such happy news made up for all the fatigues of his voyage.

We spent two months together at New Orleans, waiting for French ships to arrive, and set sail at last and landed a fortnight ago at Havre. As soon as I landed I wrote to my family. In my brother's reply I learned the sad news of my father's death, which I have only too much reason to fear was hastened by my follies. The wind was favourable for Calais, and I at once took another ship in order to go to the house of a relative of mine a few leagues from this town, where my brother writes that he will be waiting to meet me.

NOTES

1. Horace, *Ars Poetica*, lines 42–44:

   > Arrangement's virtue and value reside, if I'm not wrong,
   > In this: to say right now what's to be said right now,
   > Postponing and leaving out a great deal for the present.

   The classical aesthetic here expressed claimed for its inspiration Horace and subsequently Boileau (*Epistle VI*). It is less the aesthetic of the Man of Quality than of Prévost himself, speaking here through his narrator.

2. This preamble refers us back to the beginning of volume III of the *Mémoires d'un homme de qualité*, whose departure for Spain dates from July 1715; the encounter at Pacy must therefore take place in February 1715. However, the internal chronology of the novel is not always exact: at the end of the narrative the departure for Le Havre ought properly to take place in the spring.

3. Passy, or Pacy-sur-Eure, not far from Evreux, was not on the direct route from Paris to Le Havre, though convoys of deportees would sometimes pass this way to avoid crowds. Numerous incidents had broken out during the deportation of prostitutes in 1720. Prévost seems here to be describing a minor incident of the kind; deportations of small groups to Louisiana had been taking place since the end of the 17th century.

4. This can be dated as early summer 1712; des Grieux completes his philosophical studies at college by taking part in publicly-held debates.

5. These coaches were heavy covered wagons, providing transport between Arras and Amiens; they were fitted with large baskets in front and behind for luggage.

6. The post-chaise was a light two-seater carriage harnessed to one or two horses. Leaving Amiens at 5.00 a.m., the lovers cover in one day the seventy-five miles to Saint-Denis, on the outskirts of Paris. This

Notes

particular trip was extremely rapid; on his return, des Grieux and his brother will take two days to cover approximately the same route.

7. Almost certainly the Rue Vivienne, very fashionable at the end of the 17th century and inhabited by the celebrated banker Melchior de Blair.

8. Des Grieux enrols in the Theological Faculty at the start of the academic year in October 1713. At the end of one year he makes his first public oration, as was usual for future seminarians.

9. Six thousand francs (two thousand écus) represented in the 18th century a very solid bourgeois income; but a carriage complete with two horses and a coachman would alone cost about three thousand six hundred francs. We can understand the Chevalier's reflection, a little further on: 'What worried me more than anything else was the upkeep of a carriage.'

10. From the 1680s a mania for gambling spread both at Court and in Paris. Card-sharpers and adventurers proliferated; the appearance of a fraternity of card-sharpers, the *Ligue de l'Industrie*, probably dates from the beginning of the Regency. Saint-Simon in his *Mémoires*, and Dancourt, Lesage and Regnard in their comedies, all make frequent allusion to this fashion.

11. The Prince de Transylvanie, François Rakokzy, took refuge in Paris after the failure of the revolt by the 'Malcontents' in 1713. He inhabited the Hôtel de Transylvanie, near to the present Académie Française, on the Quai de la Seine. His officers lived off the revenues of the gambling house which they had set up in the Hôtel. In 1714 the Prince retired to a monastery at Clagny. With the death of Louis XIV he was deprived of all protection in France.

12. Manon is brought to the Salpêtrière, the penal section of the Hôpital-Général. Reserved for prostitutes, the hospital was in fact a harsh and much-dreaded prison.

13. Incarceration in the monastery of Saint-Lazare, by *lettre de cachet* or by order of the Lieutenant of Police, provided a means of chastising the degeneracy of wealthy young men. Confinement was usually preceded by a spanking, and it is this humiliating punishment which des Grieux fears most.

14. At the age of twenty des Grieux has attained his legal majority, and can indeed claim his share of his mother's property. But he will only attain complete majority and have the right to marry without parental consent at the age of twenty-five.

15. The episode of the Italian prince was added to the 1753 edition, 'to fill out the character of one of the protagonists', as Prévost explained in the Note to this edition. And Manon does appear in a more favourable light as a result: loving, seductive, high-spirited; the joke she plays on the Italian is moreover entirely disinterested.

16. A parody of *Iphigénie*, Act II, sc. v, lines 674–82.

17. The Rue Saint-André-des-Arts runs from the Place Saint-Michel to the Carrefour de Buci, very near the Comédie Française. The play would begin at 5.00 p.m. and end at 9.00 p.m.

18. In the 1731 edition, eight days elapse between des Grieux's sending the letter to his father and the latter's arrival in Paris. In the 1753 edition, Prévost extends to several weeks the period during which the lovers are together, at the beginning of Part Two, but he forgets to delay by as much the arrival of des Grieux's father and continues to speak of 'eight days'.

19. These asterisks may refer to actual people: the Duc de . . . is perhaps the Duc d'Orleans, the future Regent; the man who lives faithfully with his mistress is perhaps the Marquis de Ferriol, who appears in Prévost's *Histoire d'une Grecque moderne* (1740); the Duc de Gesvres and the Prince de Carignan were famous for amassing fortunes from gambling. But Prévost is too prudent to name such powerful figures, whose heirs might have taken up their defence.

20. In 1718 the *Compagnie d'Occident* called upon volunteers to colonize Louisiana. Faced with the lukewarm reception of this appeal, recourse was made, from 1719 onwards, to 'unsatisfactory subjects' who were sent out by force. New Orleans was only founded subsequently. The Père de Charlevoix, historian of 'la Nouvelle-France' and a friend of Prévost, went there in 1722 and saw 'hundreds of hovels'.

21. Georgia did not as yet exist, and Florida still belonged to Spain. Des Grieux can only make for Carolina, to reach which he would have to cross the Appalachian mountains and cover over eight hundred miles.

22. The 1731 text is more explicitly Christian in inspiration: des Grieux, filled with 'the light of grace', turns back to God and practises penance. The 1753 version appeals only to a rather abstract religious impulse and to the Chevalier's aristocratic honour.

CHRONOLOGY

1697 *1 April*: Birth of Antoine François Prévost in Hesdin, second son of Liévin Prévost, public prosecutor for the King in Bailliage d'Hesdin, and Marie Duclay.

1711 *August*: Death of Prévost's mother (aged forty-two); his two sisters, Thérèse (thirteen) and Marie-Anne (three) die the same year.

September: Completes his studies at the Jesuit College in Hesdin; returns to Paris with his elder brother, Liévin.

1712 *October*: Begins his studies in philosophy; his brother Liévin joins the Jesuit order.

1713 Enlisted into the army as a volunteer, where he remains until the end of the War of Succession (1714).

1714 Returns to Paris; some months spent amongst the Jesuits for a first noviciate, before fleeing to Holland.

1716 Returns to France during the amnesty declared by the Regent.

1717 *16 March*: Admitted to the Jesuit order in La Flèche for a second noviciate.

1719 Leaves the order to return to the army as an officer during the war against Spain, after which he deserts and heads to Holland.

1720 *Summer*: Returns to France.

November: Joins the Benedictine order of St Maur, seeking solace from the heartbreak of an ended love affair.

1721 *9 November*: Takes vows at Jumièges and spends the following seven years as a Benedictine monk in the Normandy province, including a year of theology in Bec-Hellouin and sojourns in the abbeys at Fécamp and Sées.

1724 Writes *Les Aventures de Pomponius, chevalier romain*.

1725 Spends a year teaching in Saint-Germer.

1727 Enters the priesthood. Called to the Convent of the Whitecoats in Paris before being transferred to Saint-Germain-des-Prés, but is soon arguing with his superiors.

1728 *15 February*: Submits the manuscript for the two first volumes of

Mémoires et aventures d'un homme de qualité for censorship, having written them the previous year, and receives approval in March and April; the work comes out over the summer.

Involved with the *Gallia Christiana*, a learned work undertaken by the monks at the abbey in continuation of work begun by Denys de Sainte-Marthe, a former member of their order. Applies unsuccessfully to be transferred to Cluny, a less strict branch of the order.

18 October: After the failed application, renounces his vows and leaves the abbey without permission.

6 November: Learning that his superiors have obtained a letter of injunction against him, he flees to England. Volumes 3 and 4 of *Mémoires et aventures* are published in the same month.

1729 Seduces Mary Eyles, daughter of John Eyles, under-governor of the South Sea Company, while employed as her private tutor.

1730 *October*: Forced to leave England. Drafts two volumes of *Le Philosophe anglais, ou histoire de M. Cleveland, fils naturel de Cromwell, écrite par lui-même* (*The History of Mr Cleveland, Cromwell's Natural Son, Written by Himself*). Returns to Holland to continue that work and sends the book to the Dutch publishing house Néaulme in December.

1731 *January–February*: Rapidly draws up volumes 5 and 6 of *Mémoires et aventures*, followed by *Manon Lescaut* (otherwise known as volume 7, *Les Aventures du chevalier des Grieux et de Manon Lescaut, par Monsieur D…*).

April: Due to being outlawed in France, the three volumes are published in Amsterdam, alongside their translated versions in London under the pen name of the 'exiled Prévost'. Returns to The Hague, and becomes romantically involved with the adventurer Lenki Ekhardt, a woman of questionable reputation.

July: Volumes 1 and 2 of *Cleveland* are published by Néaulme.

1732 *January–November*: Correspondence with Néaulme bears witness to his progressive ruin and his inability to complete *Cleveland*.

1733 *January*: Goes bankrupt, travels to England with Lenki Ekhardt, and attempts to get back on his feet by editing a weekly gazette, *Le Pour et Contre*, which is along the same lines as Addison's *The Spectator*. *December*: Issues a false cheque under the name of one of his former pupils, Francis Eyles, and is locked up in London's Gate House Prison, to be released on 29 December.

1734 *January*: Undertakes steps to rejoin the Saint Benoît order after discreetly returning to France. Receives a letter of absolution on 5 June.

1735 Obliged to carry out a second noviciate lasting several months at La Croix-Saint-Leufroy.

1736 *January*: Receives the patronage of the Prince of Conti, and is chosen as his Chaplain.

1739 *March*: Completes the manuscript copy of the final part of *Cleveland*.

1740 *February*: Bankrupt once again and in poor health. Works maniacally as a result, publishing the end of the *Doyen de Killerine, histoire morale, composée sur les mémoires d'une illustre famille d'Ireland* (begun in 1735), followed by 'L'histoire de Marguerite d'Anjou' in July, and *L'Histoire d'une Grecque moderne* in October.

1741 Forced to seek a year's exile in Frankfurt and Brussels after a scandal involving an article in one of his handwritten gazettes.

1742 *September*: Settles in Paris to work on diverse translations for the Didot publishing house: *Histoire de Guillaume le Conquerant*, and Richardson's *Pamela* (1742), *Histoire de Cicéron* by Middleton (1743) and *Lettres de Cicéron* (1744); manages to pass off his translation of 'Les voyages du capitaine Robert Lade' (1744), although fails to do the same with his version of 'Les mémoires d'un honnête homme' (1745).

1745 *January*: Didot is granted permission to compile *L'Histoire générale des voyages*, a vast compendium of English, Italian, Spanish and French travels, which Prévost translates and puts in order. Fifteen volumes appear between 1746 and 1759.

1751 Successfully publishes a translation of Richardson's *Clarisse Harlowe* (*Lettres anglaises ou Histoire de Miss Clarisse Harlowe*).

1752 Frequents the social circle of Jean-Jacques Rousseau and his friends.

1755 Publishes translation of *Nouvelles lettres anglaises, ou Histoire du chevalier Grandisson*.

1760 *April*: Settles in Saint Firmin near Chantilly with his governess, Catherine Genty. Submits volumes 1 and 2 of *Monde moral*, his last novel. Continues to publish translations of Hume, Frances Sheridan, etc. until his death.

1763 *23 December*: Dies suddenly of an aneurysm while walking in the neighbouring woods near Saint-Firmin. Buried at the House of the Benedictines in Senlis.

PENGUIN ONLINE

READ MORE IN PENGUIN

In every corner of the world, on every subject under the sun, Penguin represents quality and variety – the very best in publishing today.

For complete information about books available from Penguin – including Puffins, Penguin Classics and Arkana – and how to order them, write to us at the appropriate address below. Please note that for copyright reasons the selection of books varies from country to country.

In the United Kingdom: Please write to *Dept. EP, Penguin Books Ltd, Bath Road, Harmondsworth, West Drayton, Middlesex UB7 0DA*

In the United States: Please write to *Consumer Services, Penguin Putnam Inc., 405 Murray Hill Parkway, East Rutherford, New Jersey 07073-2136.* VISA and MasterCard holders call 1-800-631-8571 to order Penguin titles

In Canada: Please write to *Penguin Books Canada Ltd, 10 Alcorn Avenue, Suite 300, Toronto, Ontario M4V 3B2*

In Australia: Please write to *Penguin Books Australia Ltd, 487 Maroondah Highway, Ringwood, Victoria 3134*

In New Zealand: Please write to *Penguin Books (NZ) Ltd, Private Bag 102902, North Shore Mail Centre, Auckland 10*

In India: Please write to *Penguin Books India Pvt Ltd, 11 Community Centre, Panchsheel Park, New Delhi 110017*

In the Netherlands: Please write to *Penguin Books Netherlands bv, Postbus 3507, NL-1001 AH Amsterdam*

In Germany: Please write to *Penguin Books Deutschland GmbH, Metzlerstrasse 26, 60594 Frankfurt am Main*

In Spain: Please write to *Penguin Books S. A., Bravo Murillo 19, 1°B, 28015 Madrid*

In Italy: Please write to *Penguin Italia s.r.l., Via Vittorio Emanuele 45/a, 20094 Corsico, Milano*

In France: Please write to *Penguin France, 12, Rue Prosper Ferradou, 31700 Blagnac*

In Japan: Please write to *Penguin Books Japan Ltd, Iidabashi KM-Bldg, 2-23-9 Koraku, Bunkyo-Ku, Tokyo 112-0004*

In South Africa: Please write to *Penguin Books South Africa (Pty) Ltd, P.O. Box 751093, Gardenview, 2047 Johannesburg*